stopping to home

stopping to Home

Lea Wait

Margaret K. McElderry Books

New York   London   Toronto   Sydney   Singapore

Margaret K. McElderry Books
An imprint of Simon & Schuster Children's Publishing Division
1230 Avenue of the Americas
New York, New York 10020

Book design by Sonia Chaghatzbanian
The text of this book is set in Bembo.

Printed in the United States of America
2 4 6 8 10 9 7 5 3 1

Library of Congress Cataloging-in-Publication Data
Wait, Lea.
Stopping to home / Lea Wait.— 1st ed.
p. cm.
Summary: In 1806, orphaned eleven-year-old Abigail and her little
brother Seth find a home with the young Widow Chase in the seaport of
Wiscasset, Maine, and help her discover a way to support them all.
ISBN 0-689-83832-8
[1. Orphans—Fiction. 2. Brothers and sisters—Fiction. 3. Widows—
Fiction. 4. Maine—History—1775-1865—Fiction.] I. Title.
PZ7.W1319 St 200
[Fic]—dc21
00-028373

For the women of my family: my grandmothers, Caroline Eleanor and Cornelia; my mother, Sally; my sisters, Nancy and Doris; my nieces, Heather, Laura, and Katie; my daughters, Caroline, Alicia, Rebecca, and Elizabeth; and my granddaughters, Victoria and Vanessa. All of them, in different worlds, in different ways, have had to find their own places.

And with great thanks for the archives of the Wiscasset Library, for a work-in-progress grant from the Society of Children's Book Writers and Illustrators, and for the support and encouragement of Emma Dryden and Stephen Fraser of Simon & Schuster.

stopping to home

Chapter 1

Wiscasset, District of Maine
March 1806

"Don't cry, Seth. No one will take you away." I looked straight at Doc Ames. Seth's arms tightened around my waist. I could feel him shaking as he burrowed his head deep into my long petticoats and apron. "I promised Ma I'd take care of Seth. That's what I'm going to do."

"Abbie, you're a strong girl. Stronger than most for eleven. But life isn't easy. You'll be able to find service in some home in Wiscasset. But Seth is too young to work. Let him go to the orphanage in Portland. He'll learn a trade there. When you're older, maybe then you can bring him home."

Seth turned. His red curls were matted; his face swollen with tears. He looked at the doctor, and then at me. "Pa will come and take care of us, won't he, Abbie?"

His voice softened, and his shoulders slumped against me again. "Pa will come."

"Your father's been gone over six months now, Seth. There's been no word from any aboard his ship." Doc Ames shook his head. "No other relatives?"

"We have a grandmother in Baltimore." Ma had come from Baltimore. She had once said her mother might still be alive. A grandmother would want her grandchildren, wouldn't she?

I pulled the blue knit shawl tighter around my shoulders and looked once more at the room that had been home for Seth and Ma and me. And Pa, when he'd not been at sea.

There are folks who are rich and folks who are not. And my ma and pa and Seth and I, we are not. Our home was a small, low-ceilinged attic over the room where Widow Wink lived and made and sold her ginger beer on Water Street, near Union Wharf. Now the smell of ginger mixed with that of the sulfur Doc Ames had thrown on the floor to try to rid us of the smallpox, and with the salt river air that blew through the walls and the slats in the wooden shutters.

The pallet where Seth and I sometimes slept and the quilts that covered, if not warmed, us were in one corner. The table where we ate and Ma and I sewed was in the center of the room. On it was Ma's one treasure: a small female eider duck carved out of wood. A peddler for whom she had once sewn a waistcoat had given it to her. Sometimes Ma had sat and stared out over the river, stroking the wood as if it were a real bird. I looked at the duck. I didn't look into the corner where Ma lay.

Her body was on the pallet she had shared with Pa when he was ashore, and with Seth and me, for warmth, when he was not. I had already washed her with river water, combed and braided her long dark hair the way she liked, and covered her body and face with her favorite green quilt. She was my ma, but she was not beautiful, and the pox had not been kind to her. There was nothing else to be done for her now.

Doc Ames ran his hand through his long thinning gray hair. He had spent more time with us than most would have. There were others in Wiscasset who needed him. Others who could pay for his help. And it was late in the day. No doubt his wife had hot biscuits and boiled ham waiting for him. The thought of supper made my stomach rumble.

"It is too cold to leave you two here tonight. You need warmth, and you need food." He looked around. It was clear we had neither fire nor provisions.

"Come with me. Captain Chase is ill, and his young wife without help. Their kitchen girl fled to her people in Hallowell for fear of the pox. You could work for your keep, Abbie, and for now they might find a place for the boy, too. It would give you time to write to your grandmother in Baltimore."

If there were any chance Seth and I could stay together, I would take it.

I wrapped our thickest quilt around Seth and picked him up. The warmth from his body would warm me, too, at least a little. I didn't remember how it felt not to be cold. Winters are long in the District of Maine. I tucked Ma's eider duck under the quilt with Seth. We needed to take a bit of Ma with us.

Water Street was filled with red flames and black smoke. It looked like the picture of Hell in the Reverend Packard's Bible. The flames were from tar barrels filled with burning oil that people thought would kill the pox. Low mists of river fog mixed with the smoke, merging the land and water with red streaks of sunset.

"Red sky at night, sailor's delight," Pa always said. There would be fair weather tomorrow.

I carried Seth along the rough dirt and stones of the street, following Doc Ames and stumbling with Seth's weight and my weariness. The smell of burning tar filled our noses. Seth coughed deeply. I forced my-self not to cough, and shifted his weight, making him easier to carry.

Suddenly the church bells rang.

Mr. Webber, the sexton, only rang the church bells on a weekday for one reason. He rang the bells when someone in town had died.

For the past two weeks he had rung those bells five or six times a day. Doc Ames and I counted quietly together.

Three rings. A child had died. Nine rings would have been for a man; six, a woman.

We stood still. The second group of rings would tell us how old the child was.

One ring. Then another. Then another. Then silence. Three years old. I looked at Doc Ames.

"Must be Willy Bascomb; his fever went high," Doc said.

Willy Bascomb. The little boy with the dark skin and big eyes who had chased his dog through the church during services only last month. His father was a mariner, like our pa, and Willy and Seth had often played together on Union Wharf. I held Seth tighter.

"I'll tell Mr. Webber about your ma before I stop home."

"Thank you." It would take longer for Mr. Webber to ring for Ma. In January we'd opened our last jar of strawberry jelly to celebrate her thirtieth birth day.

The streets were empty but for the barrels of flames. We left the wharves on Water Street and turned up Main Street, passing Mr. Johnston's store, where we owed money, and the newspaper office, and Whittier's Tavern, where Ma had gone when she'd hoped for letters from Pa. The stage from Boston usually stopped at the tavern twice a week. But now there were white flags of sickness in front of many Wiscasset houses, and no stages stopped.

Finally, when I could hardly go farther, we turned onto Union Street. The doctor stopped in front of a large white house. It was wider than four houses on Water Street put together, and twice as tall. I had seen houses like it before. There were maybe a dozen in town, and more being built up on High Street. But never had I expected to see the inside of one.

A white flag hung over the large paneled door, as a flag had covered our door. Money did not make a difference to the pox. I thought of Ma on her cold pallet, and tears started to come.

Doc Ames looked at me sharply. "Abigail, remember. You'll need to mourn for your ma, but you can mourn as well in a warm kitchen where you'll be of use as you can in a cold room with no food."

I tried to brush away the tears without waking Seth. When you're four you can sleep anywhere, and Seth was used to sleeping in my arms.

"I can work." I stood up straight and tried to smile. I wasn't very tall, and some would say I was scrawny, but I could work as well as any my age, and better than many. I knew fire and food didn't come without work.

"If you don't make trouble, and help as you can, then they may let you stay for a time. Usually no one would take you, coming from a sick house as you do. But Mrs. Chase has had the pox herself. She's getting better, as Seth is, although she's still weak. Now she's nursing her husband."

I knew cleaning and I knew cooking and what I didn't know I could learn. The teacher at the new brick schoolhouse had said I was quick in learning. I suspected she was right. School learning was the easy kind, though. Learning to please folks was harder.

"I will do what needs to be done." I wished I'd taken the time to rebraid my tangled brown hair so I looked neater. Too late to do that now.

Doc Ames knocked on the door.

The young woman who opened it was very pale.

She had probably been pretty a few weeks ago. Now her blond hair hung loosely about her face, perhaps to conceal pox marks that were still healing, like the ones on Seth's back. She held her candlestick out toward Seth and me and then looked at the doctor.

"Mrs. Chase, I've brought you help."

I tried to look taller, and capable. It was hard, with Seth and the quilt tangled in my arms.

"The care of two children is not what I call help, Dr. Ames." Mrs. Chase wrinkled her nose and backed into the hallway of her house. She was wearing a loose white high-waisted muslin gown and shawl that made her look even thinner and paler than she was.

"We need no care but what I can give." My words slipped out as I saw her moving away from us. "I can cook and clean and sew as well. And wash and carry wood and make soap." It was our only chance. She *had* to take us.

"Shush, Abbie." Doc Ames frowned at me. "Mrs. Chase, you need help with the kitchen and with caring for the captain. Abigail and Seth Chambers here have just lost their ma. Abbie had the pox in the epidemic ten years ago. She won't get it now. She's a good nurse. She helped Seth over the fever. And their ma might have lived if she hadn't been sickly before the pox came."

Mrs. Chase looked at me and at Seth. For a few moments no one said anything. Seth whimpered in his sleep and tried to snuggle closer. The whimpers were as much from hunger as from grief or discomfort. There had been no food for two days. I had given Ma the last of the broth Widow Wink had left on the stairs for us.

Mrs. Chase finally spoke. Her voice was softer this time. "Losing your mother would be hard at any age. And you're right. I could use some help with the captain." Decision made, she turned to the doctor. "Doc Ames, please see if there's anything you can do. His fever's broken some, but the rash has started. His back is hurting him something awful."

Just like Ma had been after five or six days.

She pointed toward the left. "The kitchen's that way. There's enough beef soup on the fire and bread on the table for you and your brother." She turned toward the stairs. "There's bedding in the corner of the kitchen that Jessie used before she ran to her folks. You can use that. After you've eaten, go outside, by the back door—you'll see it—and get some wood from the pile and bring it upstairs. I'll need more logs for the captain's fireplace soon."

She headed up the circling stairs, holding her candlestick high. Doc Ames followed.

He looked back a moment and spoke softly. "It's up to you, Abbie. Each of us makes his own future."

I walked through the room to the left, carrying Seth carefully so we wouldn't touch anything. It was an elegant room, with a polished wood table and chairs. Above a mantelpiece silver candlesticks shone in the red tar barrel light coming through the glass windows.

Captain Chase and his wife had three fireplaces.

One in the kitchen, to be sure, but here was another, unused for now and that I could see was for company, and Mrs. Chase had talked of still another, upstairs in the captain's chamber. It was hard to think of such luxury. We had had no fireplace at all, just the heat from the sides of the chimney that took the hot air from Widow Wink's fire downstairs to the roof above us. She had been kind enough to let us use her kitchen for cooking each morning. But when she was not to home there was no fire and no heat.

The Chases' kitchen was large, and the fire well banked. I put Seth down near the hearth and added a bit of kindling from the pile next to the fireplace. The

fire heated up easily enough. I shivered as the warmth
entered my outstretched fingers and I realized how
cold the rest of my body was. Seth smiled drowsily at
the red and yellow flames.

The heavy iron pot on the crane was half full of
beef soup. There were even pieces of carrots and potatoes in it. I didn't wait for it to heat more. I ladled
some into a pewter porringer and broke off pieces of
dark bread from the loaf on the table.

Seth opened his mouth as soon as he saw what I
had. I sat next to him on the floor near the fire, spoon-
ing the fragrant broth into first his mouth and then my
own. When there was no more in the porringer we
wiped the bowl with the bread and ate it, every crumb.
I cannot imagine anything tasting as good as that soup
and bread.

"Seth, we are going to be warm here. We are going
to have food. And we will stay together. You must be
very good and I must work very hard and we will be
all right." I spoke to myself as much as to him. I
hugged him tightly and tucked him under the pile of
many-colored quilts and woven blankets Jessie had
left. I put Ma's eider duck on a small empty pine shelf
above the pallet.

I didn't want the captain to wait long for his wood.

As I filled my arms at the woodpile, the bells tolled again. Six rings for a woman. Doc Ames must have told Mr. Webber about Ma.

The bells were still ringing when I reached the captain's bedchamber. It takes many minutes to toll a lifetime.

Chapter 2

April 1806

"I am going to be a blue-water man, like Pa," Seth said. "I am going to sail away on the biggest schooner in the harbor! I am going to see the Indies and France and Boston!"

"Maybe someday. Now you will go outside to the pump and bring me water so I can heat it and wash up these dishes." I handed the wooden bucket to Seth. "And you will come back. Blue-water men don't always come back."

"Pa will come back," Seth said. He took the bucket and went out the back door.

The month at Captain Chase's had not been an easy one. Now the captain lay, like Ma, in the cemetery down on Federal Street. When the stonecutter was finished, Captain Chase would have a fine marble stone to mark his passing. Only a pile of smooth sea stones Seth and I had gathered near the high tide mark outlined Ma's grave. But marked or unmarked, both Ma and the captain were gone.

After the captain died I sat up two nights with the new Widow Chase sewing her mourning garments. She did the fancywork and embroidery and pleating, which she has a fine hand for, and I did the plain stitching, which I had learned from Ma. After that, Widow Chase gave me some new black homespun and helped make mourning clothes for Seth and me.

I thanked her from my heart. It showed she had respect for our ma and for Seth and me, and was a great kindness, I know.

My new black gown and aprons and Seth's shirt and trousers are the first clothes Seth and I own that someone else has not worn first.

Widow Chase lies in her pillows when there is no company. Sometimes she cries. Sometimes she just lies, looking at the wall, or works on a large embroidery of a ship done in black silk threads in memory of the captain. She has embroidered some of his long dark hair into the sails of the vessel. She is grieving, to be sure, but I think it is more than her husband's death that keeps her to her bed.

Last week, while I was serving tea, I overheard her speaking to Mr. Jonathan Bowman, her husband's lawyer.

"Lydia, you must think carefully. You are young, and you are alone. How will you be able to manage?"

"I have the house, Jonathan. Are you sure there is nothing else?"

"Usually your husband took a ship out twice a year, or even three times. Last year he only sailed in the spring."

"After our wedding, he did not wish to leave." Widow Chase smiled sadly and touched her narrow gold wedding band. "He was planning to take the *Horizon* to the Indies this month." She tucked a loose curl behind her ear. "Are you quite sure there is nothing more?"

"There is a little money in the Lincoln and Kennebec Bank. It might last you until the end of this year, or a little into next." He shook his head. "Your best course would be to sell this house and move back to your family in Augusta. You'd then have money to live well enough until you marry again."

"Marry again! Jonathan, it has been less than a

month since my husband's death. Surely it is too soon to talk of other marriages."

"Perhaps too soon for social graces, but not too early for practicality. You have no way of supporting yourself, Lydia."

"I will not go back to Augusta. There must be a way."

I heard no more, as I had to attend to Seth, who was singing too loudly in the kitchen. I know it is not polite to listen to conversations in which you are not a part, but Widow Chase's situation is of concern to me as well as to her. If she should move to Augusta, as Mr. Bowman urged her, there would be no place for Seth and me.

She is pale and thin, and I know she has been light-headed once or twice when she didn't think anyone noticed. I do the washing and the cooking and I keep my eyes open. I try to bring her small portions of food several times a day so she will eat more.

The pox epidemic is now gone from Wiscasset. Captain Chase was one of the last to die. People are beginning to come back to town, but nothing is the same as before the sickness. I hoped to return to school, but our teacher was one of those who died. There will be no more school this spring.

But I am not without activity. I must be here for Seth,

and now for Widow Chase, who depends on me. She gets herself up and dressed when friends stop in, or when the Reverend Packard visits. Those occasions come often enough to keep me in the kitchen baking most days.

The guests sip tea or wine. That is much more elegant than the cider or beer Ma used to drink. I have found Widow Chase is especially fond of sipping port wine, so I ensure it is nearby. It smells very sweet. I often wonder how Ma might have liked the taste of it. Here the widow and her friends assume the choice of food and drink is a matter of preference. In many other houses that is not the case.

I have already learned to make small fancy sweet cakes for company. They take molasses or sugar and dried fruits and nuts or seeds. They also take more patience than loaves of plain wheat or corn or anadama bread. I am getting to be quite good at baking them. Widow Chase's friends have several times complimented me on my work. That pleases Widow Chase, which pleases me. I know I must prove my worth to stay in such a house.

Seth has developed a taste for cakes, but their sweetness is too strong for me. I choke sometimes on remembering how we used to live. I bake the cakes, but I do not indulge myself.

This house is not ours; we are only waiting here until something else happens. What that something is, I cannot be sure. But I know we must not allow ourselves to be too comfortable here.

Widow Chase has seen how Seth loves the sweets and often gives him some or tells me to save some for him. If it pleases her to spoil Seth a little, I believe the noise of his running and giggling does not disturb her too much. That is important if we are to stay here. A child of four is still young enough to be spoiled without harm.

Mrs. Chase's friend Sally Clough has caused me to spend today in the kitchen. It is a fine spring day. Sparrows are twittering in the pines outside the window. Ice is almost gone from the river, and sun fills the kitchen. It is warm enough so the first of the flies are buzzing. I have to cover the food with cloths to keep the creatures away.

I would like to walk down to the harbor to see what vessels are arriving. Perhaps a mariner would have heard of Pa or his ship. But instead I am baking trays of small molasses cakes seasoned with caraway seeds and raisins.

Sally Clough is Widow Chase's closest friend. Her family lives on Jeremy Squam Island, across the Sheepscot River, and they escaped the smallpox. Tomorrow, despite most families in Wiscasset being in mourning, Sally is marrying Mr. Bowman.

"I know it is hard for you to rejoice in my happiness in the midst of your bereavement. But I just can't help thinking of the wonderful cakes you had at your wedding supper last summer. Could you find the strength to make some for Mr. Bowman's and my special day?"

Sally knew Widow Chase wasn't well enough to make cakes, and certainly no woman in such early mourning could attend a wedding. But, nevertheless, the widow had agreed to provide what Sally asked.

"Sally made cakes for my wedding, and I must help her in return," Widow Chase told me. "Someday you will ask friends to make cakes for your wedding and you will see how it is."

I thought that very unlikely.

As I made the cakes under her direction, Widow Chase fashioned a yellow silk wedding bonnet with white embroidery for Sally, which the bride had also requested.

"Sally is only sixteen and so excited about being married and moving to a big town like Wiscasset."

Widow Chase sighed as her needle produced tiny tucks covered with flowers to frame Sally's face. I believe she was thinking of her own wedding.

She had married last July. The Reverend Packard told me during one of his visits. She had been a wife only eight months before she became a widow.

I do not think much of marriage from what I have seen.

Ma's husband was seldom with her, and times when he was home he was most often at the tavern. He had time to play ball with Seth, but had hardly a civil word for Ma or me. Ma had left her family in Baltimore and come to care for him and for his mother and then for us. I could not blame her death on Pa. But she suffered it without him, and without the warmth of fireplace or family, except for Seth and me.

Widow Chase married a wealthy captain and lives in a big house. But now she is alone.

Mr. Bowman, whom Sally is to marry, although a lawyer and of considerable standing, is old. I have heard Widow Chase say he is thirty-five. He is a widower. His daughter, Louisa, who is eight, has been living with her grandparents.

Everyone in town knows Louisa. Her grandparents are General Abiel Wood and his wife. General Wood owns the largest wharf in Wiscasset and so many vessels, I've heard folks say you could cross the Sheepscot River just by stepping from the deck of one of his ships to the deck of another.

Louisa knows that well. If you have any doubt about her grandfather's importance, or her own, she will tell you. In school she wore new gowns more often than most children could memorize new lessons. I suspect she will not relish leaving her grandparents' big house or having a stepmother only eight years older than she is.

I do not envy Sally Clough her wedding.

The back door banged. Seth came in, spilling water from his bucket over the floor.

"Seth! Is it not enough that the yard is full of mud and the floor here besides, after the rain last night? Another bit of dirt and Widow Chase will be asking us to plant beans in the kitchen floor."

"Could we, Abbie?"

I laughed and took the bucket. I poured the remaining water into the kettle and hung the kettle on the crane, giving Seth a quick swat on his bottom as we both sat down on the pine bench near the fireplace.

"Have you written the letter yet? The letter to our grandmother in Baltimore?"

"Seth Chambers, you asked me that three times this morning. Yes, I wrote the letter, and, yes, I sent it."

I didn't tell Seth that writing the letter wasn't the hard part. The hard part was knowing where to send it.

Ma had spoken only briefly of her family. All I knew of her father was that he had died before she met Pa. Pa was in Baltimore working on a coaster, a small ship that carries passengers and packages from one coastal city to another.

Ma never said, but I do not think her mother thought highly of the marriage. Pa was a poor mariner, and Maine was a distance from Maryland. Ma and Pa could both read and write a little, but perhaps Ma's mother could not. I don't ever remember Ma getting a letter from her mother or sending a letter there. I had no address to write to other than the town, and no name other than Ma's, before she was married. I did have that. Her name had been Alston; Rebecca Alston.

"What will our grandmother say? Will she come get us? Will she make us leave Wiscasset?" Seth looked at me earnestly. "We should wait here. Pa will come back and find us here."

"If we leave here we will leave word for Pa at Whittier's Tavern," I promised. "That way he will know where to find us." Whittier's Tavern was also the post office for Wiscasset, and people often nailed personal notices to the walls there.

"He would miss us very much if he couldn't find us, wouldn't he, Abbie? A father would always miss his children." He paused. "Pa doesn't know how sick I was of the pox. Or that Ma died."

If Pa had loved us, he would have come home by now. Voyages to the West Indies didn't take seven months. At the very least, he could have written. Ma had hoped so for his letters that never came. "No, Seth, he doesn't. But there is no sense in thinking about such things. If Pa wants to come home, and can come home, then he will be here someday. And, if not, there's nothing we can do about it."

I gave him a hug. "But we have each other. And we have a special treat this afternoon."

Seth brightened at once.

I handed him a few of the raisins I had put aside from those intended for the wedding cakes.

He chewed them slowly, one by one, his face round and smiling. He had gained a little weight in the time we had been here. And he was already having fewer nightmares in which he cried out for Ma.

"The rest of the raisins are to go in the cakes for

Sally Clough's wedding to Mr. Bowman tomorrow. The cakes are very special. But Widow Chase has said you may eat one of them when I have finished."

"Now?"

"Not yet," I told him. "When they are finished baking."

"When you get married, will you have cakes at your wedding?"

"Don't talk silliness, Seth. I am far too young to be married. And being married is not that important. I may never get married."

"You have me," Seth pointed out. "You could marry me."

"I could not marry you. But I do have you, and you have me, and we are a family."

"Even without Ma and Pa?"

"Even without Ma and Pa. Now you go outside and stack the kindling that's fallen off the woodpile into the mud."

Seth ran outside. He loved to stomp in the mud, and April was the perfect month for that. I'd be regretting it when he came back in and brought the mud with him, but the time would allow me to wash up the bowls and pots while the cakes baked.

I got the kettle, now hot from the fire, and poured the water into the large iron pot used for washing.

Outside, I could hear Seth singing a song without words, but with joy in the spring.

I went over to our corner of the kitchen and put my hand on Ma's eider duck. "We're doing all right, Ma," I whispered. "Seth and I are going to be fine. I promise."

Chapter 3

May 1806

"Abbie, there's no reason for you to stay here longer. Take Seth and go watch the marching. Here." Widow Chase reached into her pocket and handed me a silver dollar.

I took it carefully.

"You've been working all spring. There's no reason you shouldn't have a holiday like everyone else in the District of Maine. Buy some Muster cakes and some cider, or whatever the two of you might want. And don't worry yourself about preparing dinner. There's ample for me here, and likely you'll eat more than enough during the day, so you'll not be needing supper tonight."

"Aren't you coming, too, Widow Chase?" I knew her stomach had not been well again, but no one would want to miss Muster Day!

"It's not so far to the green that I can't come along later. I think I'll rest awhile. Sally Bowman is going to stop in. I may go with her."

She would certainly rather enjoy Muster Day with her friend than with two children.

Seth pulled my hand. His feet were dancing with excitement. "Let's go now, Abbie. Now!"

"Thank you. Very much." The dollar was a very generous gift. It was more than enough to buy food and drink. It would also buy a length of new cloth for sewing, black hair ribbons for me, and a small toy or firework for Seth, besides. I slipped it into the pocket under my skirts.

"You've earned it. Now, Seth"—Widow Chase knelt down so her pale face and his freckled one were close to each other—"make sure you stay with your sister in the crowds. Don't get lost. And don't get in the way of the soldiers."

He shook his head so vigorously, his red curls bounced. "No, Widow Chase." He pulled on my hand again. "Please, Abbie. Let's go. Now!"

I hesitated. "Will you be well?"

"Well enough, Abbie. Now—go. Both of you!" She gave us each a little push.

Seth led the way, pulling on my arm as I quickly

took off my black apron and put it on its hook. We ran out the back door, across the yard, and toward the village green.

The hill in front of the church was covered with people. Ever since we won the War of Independence twenty-three years ago, all able-bodied men between the ages of eighteen and forty-five have had to meet in their towns to practice marching and drilling on the first Tuesday of every May, called Muster Day. Since the men cannot work on their farms or in their fishing boats or at their logging camps that day, they bring their families with them and the whole District has a holiday.

Seth pulled and pushed me through the crowd of women, children, and old men so he could see the drilling.

Some men wore what they could find of their old soldiering uniforms and carried knapsacks, canteens, and cartridges, just as though they were ready for war. The threadbare black jackets and old-style breeches with dark blue thick-seamed stockings hung loose on some men, and stretched seams on others, all of whom were proud to remember the days when Wiscasset men fought the English for our country's freedom. Most men did not own military dress and had just put on their everyday breeches, waistcoats, and shirts. The few who did not have firearms carried sticks.

They marched up and down the hill, waving at people they recognized in the crowd. Jason Tucker, whose father is the blacksmith, was the drummer. His drumming was loud, if not regular.

Grown men marched with pride and restraint. Younger men smiled and blushed and tried to march in the patterns their fathers set. Some men wore spruce twigs in their wide-brimmed hats. Spruce twigs were the symbol Maine men wore into battle to show their pride in the District. Maine was a part of Massachusetts, but I'd heard Pa and other men say it should be a separate state. They said Boston politicians couldn't understand the needs of mariners and lumbermen and shipbuilders on the Maine frontier.

"When I am a man I will march, too," said Seth. He picked up a small stick and put it over his shoulder.

"But now you will put the stick down." I took the stick from him. "Seth, you almost hit me in the eye."

"I will be a soldier and I will go to war!" He marched around me in circles.

"If need be, you will. But it's not a day to look forward to." I reached out to stop his circling. "We should get something to eat before everyone else does the same." We headed down Main Street from the green, walking past rows of tall elm trees covered with new spring green leaves.

Every peddler in the area had gathered in Wiscasset, and every store and tavern was open. Drilling makes men thirsty. We passed Widow Wink with her ginger beer, and several men selling glasses of rum. Some women and girls had brought small cakes or gingerbreads to market. The smells of ginger, cinnamon, and molasses mixed with the odors of many people in a small place on a warm day in May.

A few farmers' wives had brought in young calves or lambs to sell. Seth stopped to pet every lamb he saw. "Please, Abbie, can we buy a lamb?"

"There is no room for a lamb at Widow Chase's." The bleating lambs were sweet. But they also smelled considerable and took much care.

Suddenly our movement through the crowd brought us face-to-face with Louisa Bowman.

Since her father's marriage she had come once with Mrs. Bowman to see Widow Chase, and I had served tea. She knew I was in service there.

"Widow Chase let you out of the kitchen, Abbie? How kind of her."

"Widow Chase is kind, Louisa," said Seth.

"I'm sure she is. Kind enough to take in two poor orphans, after all." Louisa tried to look down at us, even though I was taller than she was.

"We are not orphans. Not any more than you," I said to her calmly. "We, too, have a father. And we are not charity wards. We work for our keep."

"I'm sure you do. And perhaps you have a father. But, if you do, then where is he?" She made a show of looking in every direction. "He doesn't seem to care enough to stay around." Louisa fluffed the lavender sash on her white gown. "Or maybe he has drowned, or his ship has been seized by pirates, or he has been impressed by the English navy." Her sash matched her lavender hair ribbon, and she was wearing fine white leather shoes. "I heard my new mother say Widow Chase might move back to her folks in Augusta. And that, in any case, the regular hired girl would be back soon, since the pox is over. Then what will happen to you?"

"Don't say things about our pa," Seth yelled, his hand clutching mine. "Our pa is coming home. We won't need Widow Chase, or anyone."

"May be, Seth. Time will tell. It must be hard to be so poor." Louisa patted his red curls lightly, smoothed her skirts, and walked toward a group of girls giggling at a boy trying to walk on his hands.

"Pa will be home soon, Abbie, won't he?" Seth looked at me. "I'm not an orphan, am I?"

"No. You are not an orphan." But why hadn't we heard from Pa? It was getting harder and harder to answer Seth's questions. If Pa wasn't coming back, why didn't he write and say so? Any word would be easier than not knowing. But the moment had to be attended to. I pushed my feelings about Pa to the back of my mind. "Seth, you look like a boy who could eat a cinnamon cake. What do you think?"

"Do they have cinnamon cakes with raisins? Like wedding cakes?"

"If they do, then we're going to find them." I put my arm around him. "We're going to find everything we need."

Widow Chase was still in much discomfort the next morning. I fixed Darjeeling tea and thin slices of anadama toast for her and then asked permission to go greening.

"I would take Seth with me, Widow Chase. We would not go far. I know some places just north of town. Fresh dandelion greens and fiddleheads would do you good. We could be back in time to prepare dinner, and the house would be quiet so you could rest this morning. Sometimes Seth's voice can be loud."

She looked very tired and pale. "Yes, his voice can be loud. He is a little boy. But his sounds are happy ones. You are a good sister to him, Abbie." She set aside the floral embroidery she was working.

"It is a good idea for you to go greening. The day is beautiful, and you and Seth could get outside for a few hours. We would all benefit from what you can gather, and the dandelions might steady my stomach."

We found many new leaves of dandelions, small enough so they were not yet bitter, and a mess of fiddlehead ferns in the damp ground near a stream. The Abenaki Indians showed colonists how to value fiddleheads. We did not get enough to pickle, as some folks do, but our basket was heavy enough. I also sought out the leaves of the betony plant, as Ma had shown me.

I cooked the dandelion greens in a little water with a piece of salt pork, and we had them for dinner, with baked beans. Widow Chase joined us in the kitchen for the meal. She ate heartily of it all despite her earlier indisposition. "Excellent cooking, Abbie. The greens were a good thought."

"Ma cooked us greens in May," Seth said with his mouth full. "Ma said they tasted of spring."

"And so they do." Widow Chase turned to me. "Have you heard anything from your father or your grandmother?"

Louisa had been right. Widow Chase wanted us gone.

"No. Nothing from either."

"Be sure to tell me when you do hear."

"I will."

Widow Chase looked over at the shelf above the pallet, where the eider duck sat. I had left the betony there. "What is that you've gathered?"

"Betony, Widow Chase."

"I don't know that green. Is it eaten like dandelion leaves?"

"No. It is crushed, and then boiled with sugar into a syrup. Ma made it every spring, for herself twice, and then for others. They do so in Baltimore, where she was born."

"And its purpose?"

I looked down at my hands, so as not to be thought presumptuous. "It is for women who are confined. To relieve discomfort in their time."

All was quiet. I could hear Seth chewing and swallowing his beans. Perhaps I had been too bold. But the cause of Widow Chase's illness had seemed clear.

Widow Chase smiled. "Abbie, you are very observant. We could be using some of that betony after Thanksgiving this year."

I had been right! Widow Chase was going to have a baby.

And she had said "we." Maybe Seth and I would still be here when the baby came.

Chapter 4

June 1806

"Widow Chase, do I have your permission to leave the house for a few moments?" I knew it might be for more than a few moments, but it was important I go. Please, I thought. Don't let her say no.

"Has Seth disappeared again?" She frowned. She had been struggling with the ruffle on a new bonnet for the past hour, and it was not falling smoothly. "Abbie, you must keep better watch over that boy."

"Yes, Widow Chase. I know. But it will do no harm to the clothes I'm washing for them to soak a little longer. I can hope he is close by." I knew, and Widow Chase knew, that Seth had probably gone to the wharves again. If I were lucky I could find him quickly. If not, I would be gone a time.

"Go, Abbie. And make it be the last time he must be brought back!"

I left the house running. It was a warm day. But I could not take time to admire the blues and pinks of the wild lupine that bloomed all over town, or to search for buttercups hidden in the grass on the sides of the dirt road. The streets were full of men and women doing their shopping, carrying on business, and gossiping on corners. I dodged an oxcart full of newly cut pine shingles, and almost ran into a brown and white cow being brought to market.

Seth knew the wharves well. I was not worried he would be lost. But a small boy could be overlooked so close to the water. Accidents could happen. Last summer little Jeremiah Crocker had caught his hand between a skiff and the dock, and the hand had been deformed since. And Eben Decker, who was my age, had fallen off one of the wharves and drowned before anyone realized he was missing.

There were nine wharves to search. I turned right on Water Street. Seth was usually near our old home. I headed in that direction, scanning the harbor at the same time to see where the most activity was this day.

Over a dozen large vessels were there, in addition to the usual two or three dozen smaller working boats or fishing craft. One two-masted brig had just arrived. Mariners were busy unloading crates, perhaps full of English china and leather-bound books and fine colored silks and woolens. Watermen ferried the crates to the wharves on skiffs and barges.

Other schooners had been loaded with winter-cut lumber and masts, salt cod, and barrel staves and hoops to be assembled in the Indies and used for rum or molasses. Those ships would be leaving today or tomorrow for the islands.

Piles of trunks and boxes belonging to passengers going to Portland or Boston were waiting to be put aboard the coaster at Carlton's Wharf.

There were people everywhere. Many I knew. Some had shops near or on the wharf, like Widow Wink or Mr. Tucker, the blacksmith, or Mr. Dole, the silversmith. Sailmakers, ships' carpenters, wagonwrights, ropemakers, wood-carvers—all worked on the wharves or on neighboring Water Street. Fishermen mended their nets and unloaded their catches there. Men who had brought logs down to the lumberyard on Jeremy Squam Island came to town to check for mail and news. Mariners who spoke English, French, Spanish, and tongues I did not recognize were common on the wharves. The men were of all different colors and sizes and nationalities, but all shared the skills and courage to sail deep waters.

Seth would be somewhere with them. He would be asking if any had news of Pa.

I looked around barrels and through netting; I dodged people and wagons. I ignored the amused glances of folks who found the sight of my flying skirts worth a smile or a chuckle.

"Abbie, are you looking for Seth?" I heard Mrs. Bowman over the sounds of many voices, the creak of masts and ropes, and the thuds of dories hitting the docks. She stood talking to her younger sister, who must have rowed their skiff over from her home on Jeremy Squam.

"Yes." I took a deep breath and realized I had a pain in my side from the running and the worry.

"I think I just saw him, over near Johnston's Wharf. He was talking to a mariner there."

"Thank you." I turned and headed toward Johnston's Wharf. It is at the far end of Water Street, near the sail lofts, ropewalks, and shipyards. That is where vessels are put into the water when they are new, or taken out of it when they need repairs or ice floes are gathering on the river. Johnston's Wharf is also the closest to the lumber mill. At this time of year work was at the mill, not in the woods. It is easier to fell trees and move them in the winter, when snow covers the brambles and bushes.

Seth was still there. He was sitting on the top of a piling on the edge of the wharf, talking with a tall, dark-skinned young man whose long curly black hair was pulled back in the eel-skin-tied queue most mariners favored.

I was furious, and greatly relieved to see him. If he had not been so close to the water I would have yelled at him in a manner most unseemly.

"Seth!" My hair had come unfastened, and I was still catching my breath. "Why did you run off again? Widow Chase was not happy for me to leave the washing to come to find you. You could have met with an accident or been lost. You must stay closer or I shall have to tie a rope between my waist and your wrist."

Seth jumped down off the piling and tried to hide behind the tall young man. I reached out and tried to get hold of him, but the mariner was between us. He was not much older than me.

"Has this young man been missing?"

"Indeed he has. And he knows well not to wander down to the wharves alone."

"Abbie, I just wanted to ask about Pa." Seth peeked out around the mariner's wide dark brown trousers. He did not look repentant.

"The ship he sailed on—it was the *Fame*? The *Fame*, out of Wiscasset?" the mariner asked.

"Yes. It sailed early last September, before the seas were high. For Barbados."

"Well, I saw the *Fame*. Some months back it was, though, in Charleston. It had gone aground and was in for repairs. Must have been January or February."

That was near the time Ma had fallen ill with the pox.

"Would you know if Stephen Chambers was with the crew?"

"No, miss; no way I'd be knowing that. I remember the ship because I thought the name was proud and because I was looking for a ship bound for Maine." He gestured toward a schooner out in the harbor a ways. "I found one. But I stopped in a number of ports before anchoring here."

"Well, we thank you, truly, for the news." I reached for Seth's hand. "Although we should not have been down on the wharf bothering folks."

"No trouble. I know what it's like to miss a pa," the mariner said. "My pa was a mariner, too."

"Did he come home?" Seth came out from behind him and looked up trustingly.

The young man hesitated. "Many times he did. I hope your pa does the same."

"What is your name?"

"I'm Noah Brown. Maybe I'll be seeing you again in town. I'll be staying for a time. But now I think your sister—she is your sister, am I right?—your sister will be wanting to get you home."

"Thank you, Noah. Thank you very much." I took Seth's hand and headed back up Water Street. Seth turned and waved. I walked faster, and he had to run to keep up.

"I'm sorry, Abbie. Really. But the picnic is next week. I hoped Pa would be there to see me run in the race."

"Seth, I will be there. You will have someone watching you."

There had been no classes at the school since the smallpox epidemic had begun. But every June there was a town picnic at the school building with games and prizes for all of the children. This year the Reverend Packard had planned the day. For the past two weeks Seth had been running around and around Widow Chase's house practicing for the races.

"I wanted Pa to be there."

"I know, Seth."

"Other boys will have their pas there."

"Some will. Some boys have fathers who are at sea, like yours, or who are away elsewhere. Not everyone will have a pa there."

"Most will."

We walked slower now, up the hill that took Main Street from the river to the green, and to the Congregational Church, which looked out over all of Wiscasset and its harbor.

"Most boys will have a pa to see them run."

I squeezed Seth's hand. "Let's ask Widow Chase if we can go clamming tomorrow. Low tide is at sunrise. It would be a good time for clams and wouldn't take me away from work in the house."

"Yes! I like to dig clams. I will get very muddy. And we will have clam fritters for dinner!"

"Likely," I answered. "Both muddy feet and clam fritters. Very likely."

"Tomorrow will be a good day." Seth's red hair shone in the sun. "And after we dig clams, I will practice running. Pa might be home by next week."

Chapter 5

July 1806

Seth asked again, "What did the letter say? What did it say about Grandmother?"

Widow Chase sat quietly in her red-painted pine rocker by the kitchen window. Her stomach was no longer upset, and she had more color in her face. This morning she was piecing a baby quilt from sections of the captain's blue shirt and of the soft green dress she had worn at her wedding. "This baby will be warmed by wool that has warmed his father and his mother. The baby will wake to see the blues and greens that are the colors of Maine." Blue for the sky and water; green for the pinewoods. It was going to be a beautiful quilt. Widow Chase pieced only one section each day, as though to make the project last.

"Abbie has already told you, Seth."

"I know. But I want to hear it again."

I rested for a moment from kneading the bread. It was hot, even this early in the morning. And the kitchen fires had to be high to bake the bread and puddings I was making.

"The letter was not from Grandmother. The letter was from a neighbor who had known her. She saw my letter to Grandmother posted on the 'unknown people' wall at the post office and took it, hoping to help. The neighbor wrote that Grandmother married again several years ago and moved to the west, to Ohio. The neighbor did not know the name of the man, or the name of the place in Ohio. She wrote she was sorry."

"O-hi-o. Is that far?"

"Very far, Seth."

"Then Grandmother will not know about us? She will not want us to come?"

"Grandmother will not know about us. She will not want us to come."

"Then we will wait for Pa here."

"You may do that, Seth," said Widow Chase.

Seth turned back to the small rounded sea stones he was shaping into an "S" on the wide pine boards of the kitchen floor.

"It is lucky for me that you are both here to help with the house and to keep me company. Jessie stayed with her family in Hallowell, and without the two of you I would have been alone. Until the baby comes."

I hoped all would be well. With babies, sometimes it is not. Many mothers do not allow themselves to love a baby until it has been wellborn and lived a time. Widow Chase loved this baby now. I wondered if our ma had loved us that much, that soon.

Widow Chase finished her piecing, and we spent the rest of the morning baking bread, puddings, and blueberry pies. We also put aside quarts of blueberries for drying on trays in the attic. They would be for pies next winter. I hoped Seth and I would be there to make them and eat them.

Yesterday was so hot we only ate pie and pudding for dinner, and drank much cider and tea and lemonade.

"This afternoon we deserve a holiday." Widow Chase stood up and stretched, and you could see that her baby was growing under her black skirts. "Let's go down to the Sheepscot and see if there are any river breezes. Perhaps we can find a fisherman to sell us some mackerel. Mackerel would make a good supper on a hot night."

"Yes, let's go!" Seth was always ready for a holiday.

Main Street was still in the heat. A few men sat in front of the stores and taverns drinking beer or rum or cider. Even the wharves off Water Street were quieter than usual.

"Look, there. Something is happening!" Seth pointed down Water Street toward Johnston's Wharf, where a small crowd had gathered.

Widow Chase grabbed his hand before I could. "We will all go together to find out what it is," she said.

Seth squirmed a bit, and pulled, but the widow kept hold of his hand, and I took the other one. The three of us walked together down Water Street. Ma and Seth and I used to walk that way. After a few minutes I dropped Seth's hand. Widow Chase was holding him well enough. There was no need for both of us.

The lumbermen standing at the end of the wharf parted as we came up, letting us through.

"Oh," Seth said softly. He knelt at the end of the wharf and looked down at the skiff floating just above the mudflats on the low tide. "Oh, he is beautiful. Where did he come from?"

In the skiff was a long-legged reddish-brown moose calf. His head was big, his nose even bigger, and his eyes were dark brown. A rope around his neck was tied to the stern of the boat. He threw his head back, straining at the rope, and "Mooooed," almost like a cow. But the sound was wilder.

One of the lumbermen spoke up. "Found him up-river some, where we were marking trees for next winter's cutting. Calves usually stay close to their mothers for a year or two, but this one was alone. His mother must have met with some accident."

The poor calf. Moose meat was good eating. I had little doubt what must have happened to his mother.

Widow Chase looked down at the small moose. "How sad for the calf. Will it eat or drink?"

"We gave it some milk, before, and some water. Seemed hungry enough."

"What are you going to do with it?"

"Haven't decided. It'll die by itself. But there's no good place for a moose close to people."

The moose calf's back legs suddenly collapsed, leaving him sitting awkwardly in the stern of the boat, trying to balance himself with the gentle movement of the skiff in the water.

"Can we take him?" Seth asked. "I could give him milk and grass. He could live in our yard."

"Afraid that wouldn't be enough for this fellow. A moose needs a lot of space. And he'll be getting mighty big, too. Taller than a horse." The lumberman grinned and gestured high above his head.

We all just looked at the young moose. He was gasping now, and moaning softly, like a sick child.

"I think I'll be taking him back upriver with me. Find him a good swamp to live in. Let him try life on his own."

"But you said he couldn't live on his own," I blurted. Rope had rubbed the moose's neck raw, leaving the bare, cracked skin exposed. "He looks sick."

"He'll be fine." The tall lumberman who had found the moose laughed. "Maybe I will keep him for a while. For a mascot."

"He looks hungry. He looks thirsty. Can we give him something to eat?" Seth looked up at the man.

"No need. Wild animals can do without for a long time." He looked at his comrades. "Not men, though. It's a stinking hot day. Who'll join me at Whittier's for some refreshment?"

The crowd of men turned away and headed for the tavern.

For a long time we stayed at the end of the wharf, watching the calf.

He looked miserable.

"Can he drink the river water? He looks thirsty."

"No; the Sheepscot is a tidal river. The water is salt."
Widow Chase bent down and touched Seth's shoulder.
"Come along, Seth. There is nothing we can do here.
Abbie, let's go and see if we can find some of those
mackerel we were wanting."

"Can't I stay with the moose?"

"No, Seth. He's a sad creature, but we cannot help
him."

Seth rose slowly. "I think he would be a good pet.
He could be my friend. I would call him Moses."

"That's a strange name for a moose," I said.

"Ma used to tell us the story of the baby Moses
who was found alone in a river. The baby moose was
found alone, too."

"I don't think naming the moose will help him."

"He should have a name. His name is Moses."

We all walked back along the wharf and down the
street, looking back occasionally.

"What will happen to him?"

"I don't know, Seth. But he is not ours to worry about."

"I think someone should worry. I don't think that
lumberman is worrying."

"No," said Widow Chase. "He should not have
taken the calf unless he was willing to care for it."

We had mackerel for supper, and very fresh and sweet they were, too. But we were all quiet, thinking.

In the morning, very early, there was a pounding at the back door.

I pulled a shawl over my shift and pushed up the latch. Noah Brown, the young mariner who had befriended Seth, was standing just outside.

"Noah?" I looked at him blankly. Seth joined me at the door, rubbing his eyes.

"Sorry to bother you, miss. I asked where you lived. I wanted you to know at home, not on the wharf, because of the boy."

"Know what?"

"The *Fame* came in about an hour since."

Seth gave a shout of joy. "Pa!"

But Noah's face said something different.

I put my arm around Seth's shoulders. "Pa isn't on the ship, is he?"

"No. I inquired for him, since Seth here has been asking people for so long."

We were orphans after all. I could feel it.

Noah saw what I thought. "No, no, Miss Abbie. I've heard nothing of his death." He hesitated. "A man on the *Fame* told me Stephen Chambers got into a fight with one of his mates. He left the ship in Jamaica. Said he would find a berth elsewhere."

I could believe Pa had been fighting. It would not have been the first time. Seth looked from one of us to the other. "Where is Pa, then? Why isn't he here?"

"He's on another ship now, Seth," I explained. "He won't be home just yet."

"But he will come home soon."

"Perhaps, Seth."

"Abbie, let's go see Moses. Before breakfast. Let's go now."

"Moses?" Noah asked.

"The moose calf that one of the lumbermen found upriver and had in a skiff at Johnston's Wharf yesterday. Seth named him Moses."

Noah bent down so he was closer to Seth. "I'm afraid Moses isn't there anymore, Seth."

"Why not?" Seth's eyes were wide. "He was there yesterday."

"He was. But the man caring for him spent a long night at the tavern and forgot to give Moses enough to drink in the heat." Noah looked almost as sad as Seth did. "He died, Seth."

Seth's tears started, and mine did, too, I will say.

Noah backed away from the door. "I am sorry to bring you such news. But I wanted you to hear about your pa where you were away from folks' eyes."

"Thank you, Noah. You are a friend."

"I'll keep looking and asking folks about your pa."

After Noah left, Seth ran to our pallet on the floor and threw himself down. He lay sobbing, pounding his fists and kicking as he shook his head. "It isn't fair. It wasn't his fault. Why didn't the man take care of him? How could he leave Moses alone like that? How could he do that?"

I sat next to Seth and gently put one hand on his heaving shoulders. "I don't know, Seth." I reached for Ma's eider duck. I put it in my lap and held both it and Seth tight. "I just don't know."

Chapter 6

August 1806

Low waves lapped at our feet as Seth and I sat on a driftwood log just above the high tide mark on the mudflats north of town. Seth had rolled up his trousers, and I pulled my dark skirts almost to my knees. The shallow water was warm in the sun, and no one was about.

Here the water wasn't deep enough for brigs or schooners, even at high tide. At low tide it was good for clamming. It was high tide now; in a few minutes the tide would turn, and our feet would be dry. We listened to the screeching of gulls circling returning fishing boats. Seth splashed his feet a little. I had spent the morning churning butter, and my arms and shoulders ached. It was good to sit at a distance from the village watching a long-legged blue heron pick his way carefully through the sea grass.

"School will start again soon, won't it, Abbie?"

"Yes; school will start in a few weeks." We had heard last week that the town had found a new school-teacher. The term could begin in September, as usual.

"This year I'm going to learn to read, Abbie. Aren't I going to learn to read?"

"I hope so, Seth." Seth was almost five now and knew all his letters and numbers. He could write them down, too. I made sure he practiced during the summer so he wouldn't forget. He had drawn letters and numbers in the dirt of Widow Chase's backyard, and had formed them out of stones and sticks. But he couldn't read much more than his name. "This year you'll be reading. And doing sums, too."

Seth nodded. "I will learn to read and write. Then, when I'm a mariner like Pa, I can send letters to you and you can send letters to me."

Pa can read and write, I thought, but no letters have come from him in almost a year. He sailed when the fields were yellow with goldenrod. Now golden-rod was beginning to bloom again.

"Seth, there are other jobs you could have. You could be a lumberman and travel deep into the woods to fell trees for masts and for building. Or be a farmer and grow corn or wheat or squash. Or you could learn smithing, or printing, or you could work at the shipyards."

"Pa is a mariner. I want to be a blue-water mariner."

"You could buy your own boat and be a fisherman. You could sail the rivers and harbors of New England and go down to the outer banks of Newfoundland for cod."

Seth shook his head. He dreamed of being like his pa. I only hoped his life would not bring me the sorrow Pa's had. But there were good men as well as bad in all professions. It was not worth the arguing now. Seth wouldn't have to decide his future until he was ten, or perhaps even twelve.

"Abbie, are you going to school this year?"

"I haven't talked with Widow Chase about it." It would be a hard fall for the widow if I were in school for part of each day. Especially with the baby coming. "I'll try to talk with her tonight." There was no other help to be had, and that was good. It meant I was needed; that Seth and I had a place as long as Widow Chase stayed in Wiscasset. But I would miss going to school. "If I can't go to school myself, I'll take you, and you must tell me everything that happens there."

"I can teach you, like you showed me my letters!"

"Yes."

We sat for a while more, listening to the water and the gulls and the crickets singing in the fields. The sun was warm on our heads. I could feel it even through the straw bonnet Widow Chase had made for me.

Straw hats are a new fashion. Mrs. Bowman saw them in Boston when she went there with Mr. Bowman on a coaster last month. Widow Chase bought straw and has been trying to form hats and bonnets out of it. She has never worked with straw before, and it cuts her hands. My bonnet wasn't the best she had made; it was for practice. I was proud to wear it, but today I took it off and held it in my lap. I wanted to soak in the sun, holding its warmth for the cold days to come.

That night, after I washed up the supper dishes, I asked Widow Chase about school. "The school starts in three weeks. Seth is excited about learning to read."

"Seth can go, of course, Abbie." She tousled his hair as he sat beside her on the floor, rolling a clay marble along a crack between two boards in the floor. "I thought we could make you a new shirt before classes begin, Seth, and buy you a new pair of shoes. It is a long walk to the schoolhouse."

"Shoes for school!" Seth stretched his bare feet out and tried to pick up the marble with his toes.

"Abbie, can you read and write?"

"Yes. I like to read."

"That is good. Reading will stand you in good stead throughout your life. And ciphering, too. Every woman needs to be able to keep household accounts. And business accounts, should her husband be away from home." She paused. "Your mother taught you to sew and to cook, and I've tried to teach you more of those skills."

"You have. Cooking, especially. I can cook almost anything now."

"But there is always something more to learn. Abbie, you want to go to school this fall, don't you?"

I looked down.

"Most folks would say a girl your age who can read and write doesn't need to sit with the little children in school anymore."

"That is true. I know. But there is so much more I want to learn! About what has happened in the world before we were in it, and about places far away, and about how other people live."

"I went to school myself until I was fourteen. In Augusta, where I grew up, there was a school for girls as well as a town school. I learned those things you are thinking of, and a little of music and art and poetry, besides."

She touched the front of her gown. I knew she was thinking of her baby. "I was very lucky. I had two parents to watch out for me."

I swallowed hard. I did not have two parents to watch out for me. I had to work. "I know you need me to help here, especially with the baby coming." My eyes stung, and I blinked quickly to rid myself of the tears. "I don't need to go to school anymore. You have been so kind to let Seth and me stay with you. It is selfish of me to think of school at my age."

Widow Chase sighed. "Abbie, I do need you. I need you very much to help me during the next few months." She paused. "But there are many ways to learn. In the parlor I have the books from my time in school, and more that my father bought me and that were my husband's. Perhaps we could read them together a little every day, after our chores are done. We could have our own small school here at home."

Without thinking, I ran and hugged her, baby and all.

"That would be wonderful!" I realized what I had done and stepped back, quickly. But she was smiling. "You would teach me at home? Really?"

"Really. And as you read the books it will remind me, too, of life outside of Wiscasset."

Seth looked from one of us to the other. "Can you teach me, too? Can I come to your school at home?"

"No, Seth," Widow Chase answered. "It is time for you to be with other children and learn to put letters together to make words. By the time you are Abbie's age you may also be leaving school to work for someone who will teach you a trade. Abbie can learn many things she will need to know as a woman right here, with me. Maybe we can both learn some things." She picked up Seth's marble as it rolled toward the door. "Tomorrow we will go to the cobbler and have him measure your feet for shoes. It will be getting cold soon enough."

"I'll knit new socks for you to wear with your shoes. And every day I will make you dinner to eat at school," I added.

Seth wiggled his toes. His feet were dark and hardened by summer roaming. "New shoes would be very good, wouldn't they, Abbie?"

"New shoes would be very good," I agreed.

I wondered what books Widow Chase would find for us to read. Maybe some of them would be about cities like Boston or New York. Or about people who lived in castles and had adventures far from New England.

Ma always said, "Some things you learn from books and some things you learn from life." At Widow Chase's I was going to learn some of each. That was more than a girl from a room on Water Street should hope for in life. Both my head and my hands had much to learn. In a few months I would be twelve, and many girls married at sixteen or seventeen.

I knew I must make the most of the life I had been given and not waste time in idle dreaming. But sometimes it was hard not to hope for more, especially when living with Widow Chase made life seem full of possibilities.

What if Pa came home and we had to leave here? This was still a temporary place, and I couldn't count on its lasting.

Not a moment must be wasted.

"I'm going to start knitting those socks for you right now, Seth." I pulled carved wooden needles and blue yarn from the knitting basket in the corner.

"Can they have red stripes on them? Blue socks with red stripes!"

"They can have red stripes on them." I tickled Seth's foot with my needle. "Big red stripes, to match those big toes of yours."

I kept thinking of those books in the parlor case. How long would it take to read them all? How long would Seth and I be here?

Chapter 7

September 1806

Mr. Johnston pulled the bolts of wool from the ceiling-high rack onto the low maple counter so the light from his store window would fall directly on them. The reds and pinks and blues and purples shimmered as the light changed.

I could choose only one. It was like trying to choose one band from the rainbow, or one wildflower from the field. It was an impossible task.

I reached out to touch one red. It felt as soft as a baby. "It's so deep and smooth. And I'm sure it would be warm enough. It would."

Widow Chase picked up the corner of the fabric and held it between her fingers. "It is thick enough and would hang well." Decision made. "We'll take four yards of this red, Mr. Johnston, and six of the white."

With Seth in school I was now spending more time with Widow Chase. As she had promised, we were reading her books. Usually I read aloud while she sewed for the baby or did some fancywork Mrs. Bowman or one of her other friends had asked her help with. Today we were choosing material for baby clothes and bedding for the cradle. Blankets would be needed, and gowns and caps and clouts, which a child would wear until he or she could use a chamber pot. I had already knit a pile of small socks and leggings and tiny warm bonnets to keep away the wind.

Most folks would just use scraps from other sewing for a baby's necessities, but scraps weren't good enough for Widow Chase's child.

"I don't care how crazy Jonathan Bowman says I am. I have some money left and I'm going to spend it on my baby." No other baby in town would have red embroidered wool blankets, but the material was beautiful and it was wonderful to sew on a color other than black. "No baby should have to wear mourning, no matter that his father has been dead less than a year. The women of the church can talk if they want to."

Already Widow Chase and I had each made Seth a

new shirt for school, and I was working on a black coat that would keep him warm when winter winds came. The widow was sewing him a small dark waistcoat. She was going to give it to him as a surprise on his birth day, in two weeks. I hoped to finish his coat by then, too. Seth would be a very elegant five-year-old.

I wished Ma could see Seth. He had grown so much during the six months we had been with Widow Chase.

I had grown myself, and so had widened some seams in my shift. Widow Chase taught me how to do it so the letting out did not show much. She said I shall soon be needing stays, but I think not. I wear a kerchief around the neck of my gown and I stand tall and hold myself in. That should prevent others from thinking of needs for stays. Some women in town have stays laced so tightly they cannot bend to pick up a dropped needle. My duties allow no time for such pretensions. And, in truth, I have no interest in putting on the garb of a grown woman before it is necessary for modesty's sake. It is hard enough to be a girl of eleven. I must take care of Seth, help Widow Chase, and always have the question of Pa's return over my head. I have no desire to hurry the time when I must make decisions about my life as a woman.

There is less and less sun each day as the darkness

of winter approaches. We have supper at four in the afternoon now so the cooking and cleaning up may be done in the light. After supper, when the candlelight is low, I am knitting wool stockings for us all. The swallows have begun to leave for warmer climates, and leaves on the maple trees and blueberry bushes are turning red. We'd be having the first frost of the season any day now. Soon enough we would be wearing wool and wishing for spring.

Our lives have fallen into a comfortable pattern. In the morning I rise early, build up the fire, knead dough for the day's bread, and prepare pie or pudding for our breakfast and something for Seth to eat at school during the nooning hour. By six I wake Seth to wash and dress and sweep out the kitchen and eat. Then I walk with him to the school so he is there by eight. It is only a mile, but Seth is not too old to want my company, and I am glad of the walk.

The first time I left him at the school was difficult, both in my leaving and in his staying. When I was little I loved sitting on the school benches with the other children, knowing that the teacher didn't care whether I lived on Water Street or High Street. And, in truth, I was proud to answer faster than those who wore more petticoats or had fuller lunch pails. Memo-

rizing multiplication tables was easier than being polite to those who laughed at the garments Ma made
over for me, or who held their noses and said I
smelled of ginger beer.

Seth will be teased about Pa's absence and about
living to Widow Chase's, no doubt. But he is dressed
as the other children and he no longer smells of ginger beer. He will manage, as I did. It is time for me to
be elsewhere. Widow Chase was right. Most of the
children in school now are younger than me.

Now after I leave Seth at school each morning I
look forward to returning to Union Street. There I
bring in the wood we will need for the day, and
Widow Chase and I finish the baking or cooking and
do the chores. Mondays we wash any clothes needing
it; Tuesdays, when these are dry, I iron them. Wednes-
days we use the birch broom to sweep out the entire
house, not just the kitchen and hall, and do other
household chores, such as airing quilts before the
winter, or polishing pewter or silver. Thursday Widow
Chase has reserved for special tasks, like making candles or soap, Friday is a day for making pies for the
week, and Saturday we work on large sewing projects
that require two of us, such as a quilt we are making
for the guest chamber. Sunday, of course, we attend

the Congregational Church, as do most people in Wiscasset. I have heard there are churches of different types in other parts of Maine, but in Wiscasset we have only the Congregational, and it serves all well.

In the afternoons, before Seth returns home full of school stories and energy, Widow Chase takes one of her books from the case in the parlor and I read aloud to her as she sews for an hour or, if I am lucky, two.

The first week Seth was in school we read a sermon by a Massachusetts minister, the Reverend Jonathan Edwards. He believed that all people are sinners and that God must punish them. I thought often that week about my sins and one night awoke with sweats and nightmares. After that Widow Chase and I agreed we are not perfect, but that we do not need to read about sins and Hell in such lengthy detail. We preferred the Reverend Packard's sermons, which talk of sins but also of the love and goodness in people.

Now we are reading the poetry of Mr. Robert Burns. He is Scottish, and his words are difficult to read on a page, but out loud they are beautiful. Yesterday I read:

But pleasures are like poppies spread,
You seize the flow'r, its bloom is shed;

Or like the snow falls in the river,
A moment white—then melts forever;

Both Widow Chase and I cried a little at the sadness of losing people in our lives. But when the snow falls in the river it gives strength to the river and to the oceans beyond. So Mr. Burns's verse is not entirely sad.

After we finish this book Widow Chase has promised we may read *Wieland,* a novel by Mr. Charles Brown that takes place in America rather than in Europe, as most novels do. Mrs. Bowman obtained a copy of *Wieland* on her last trip to Boston and, as Mr. Bowman will not let her keep it in his house for fear Louisa will be tempted to read the pages describing ghosts and murders, she has given it to Widow Chase. I am most eager to begin it, and very pleased I am thought old enough to read it without harm. Widow Chase has cautioned me not to mention this reading to anyone, for fear some townspeople would not find it suitable for either of us. Some people do not believe the reading of novels is good for the mind. I am eager to see how doing so affects mine.

Widow Chase enjoys playing schoolmistress. Once or twice Mrs. Bowman has also joined our reading and talking. I ask many questions, but they do not laugh at me. I think they value the novelty of thinking of people and places outside of Wiscasset.

Widow Chase is also teaching me some of the fancy needlework she can do so well and has allowed me some silk threads to begin a sampler to practice and show my embroidery stitches, such as fine young ladies do. At first I was not sure I could do such work, or, in truth, should even try, as my life will most likely not be one of sitting and doing gentle work while someone else takes care of the hearth. But Ma earned money sewing for women in town, and perhaps one day I can make a living that way. I know I must find a way to support Seth and me beyond the possibility of my marrying, an event that is far in the future, if ever. Should I have continued in school I might have thought of teaching, but I have no knowledge of Latin or Greek, nor am I likely to gain it, so teaching now seems unlikely. There are so few respectable ways in which a woman can make money. Sewing is certainly one, although not one of which I am fond. Some days I feel I have already sewn enough hems to last a lifetime.

I have also been learning to form hats out of straw, as Widow Chase taught herself. Because the skin on my hands is hard with frequent use, I can weave damp straw into bonnets and hats better than can Widow Chase. This work is more fun and goes faster than tiny embroidery stitches. Already she is letting me do most of the straw work. She has obtained several pictures of hats and bonnets from the Portland and Boston newspapers and says if I can copy these, she shall make the trimmings.

Six months ago I did not even know which styles were new or old. I have learned such information is very important to those who have money to indulge themselves in fashions. Widow Chase looks very pretty in a bonnet, although the black ruffles make her face look pale. In truth, she is now very healthy. It is clear the baby is growing rapidly.

Mr. and Mrs. Bowman come to dinner with Widow Chase every Tuesday. They are much concerned about Widow Chase's future, I know. I have heard them talking.

"Lydia, the time is passing. Your child will be born, and you will have nothing to pay for wood to heat your home, or food for you and the baby. Not to speak of Abbie and Seth, whom you have taken in for the moment." Mr. Bowman took another large helping of the dumplings he liked with his stew.

"Have you been in touch with your family?" Mrs.

Bowman asked, "I am so divided, Lydia. Should you return to Augusta, I would miss you very much. But, as surely, I do not want you to suffer here."

"I have no plans to return to Augusta, Sally, as you well know. But in truth I have not yet thought of an alternative."

"Your house is fine and large. You have more than enough room for you and your child. And there is need in the town for places for mariners and other travelers in port to stop. You could fill your extra bedrooms with pallets, take in boarders, and offer stew as fine as this once a day. There would surely be enough interested men away from home to support you."

Widow Chase paled. "I could not. Such men . . . in my house."

"Jonathan, of course she could not! You know the sorts of men those mariners are! Loud, and dirty, and far from home. They drink too much, they are always fighting, and many respect women and property too little."

I thought of Pa. No; Widow Chase would not be comfortable with him or his friends in this house. I knew well how loud Pa could be. The beauty of this home would only make him angry because it was not his, and because he must work for captains like Widow

Chase's husband. What would happen to us if he were to return now?

"Lydia is too gentle to be able to cope with such men," Mrs. Bowman continued. "Perhaps if there were a man here as well it would be different. But she is alone, with only two children to help her, and soon a third to care for. Making this beautiful home into a boardinghouse is no solution."

"Thank you for understanding, Sally." Widow Chase touched Mrs. Bowman's hand. "I know there must be a way to manage. And I do appreciate all of your support and ideas. But this is a problem I must solve on my own." She rose. "I am weary tonight. Would you excuse me if I must end our evening earlier than usual?"

"Of course, Lydia. I was only trying to help." Mr. Bowman rose to get his wife's cape, which I had hung in the front hall.

Despite her weariness, after they left, Widow Chase sat by herself in the parlor long into the evening.

I fear there will soon be little left in the bank and no choice for Widow Chase but to sell this house and move back to Augusta.

I have noticed that although Widow Chase finds money for the baby's blankets, we now use fewer candles and eat more beans and salt pork. Widow Chase has always bought squash and corn and beans from farmers outside of town. Last week she asked Seth and me if it would be fun for us to grow our own vegetables next summer. I think it would be much work, but it would save money, and I agreed to help her plan a garden. It is far too late this year to start anything growing. Seth, of course, was delighted at the prospect of growing his own pumpkins.

And yesterday she said, right out, "Abbie, I must find a way to support this household. I have thought and thought, but I cannot imagine a way to do so. The way you are supporting yourself and Seth." She did not mention what we both knew: that she was giving me that opportunity. "I love my family, but I do not wish to go back and live under my father's roof as a widow. When I lived there as a child and as a young woman it was my place. But now my place is out in the world. Independent."

She gets letters from Augusta often. "My mother urges me to consider the option of moving home. She has even hinted that Jason Bridges, who was once my beau, has been asking after me."

"Will your mother join you for your confinement?"

If Ma were alive I would have wanted her with me at such a time.

Widow Chase shook her head. "I have not yet mentioned my . . . situation . . . to her. I am sure if she knew she would urge me even more to come to her."

I suspected she was right. A woman should be with family when a baby comes.

Chapter 8

Late September 1806

Widow Chase and I had been sewing Seth's new clothes for several weeks while he was in school or after he had fallen asleep at night. It was her idea to give Seth his new clothes on his birth day as a surprise. Ma had never given us anything but a special hug on the anniversaries of our birth.

"In my family it was the custom to remember birth days with a gift," Widow Chase remembered. "Seth will love a surprise."

It was fun to plan the gifts and then to hide them when Seth was nearby. Sharing the secret with Widow Chase was special for me, too.

This year Seth's birth day, September 26, fell on a Friday, so Seth was at school all day. Widow Chase and

I spent the morning making Seth's favorite sesame cakes—a whole plate full, just for him. For supper I made cod chowder with potatoes and onions and salt pork, the way Seth liked it.

We put the waistcoat that Widow Chase had made for him on the kitchen table, where he would see it when he came in. Next to it I put the wool coat I had been working on for the past month. I made it long and flared, so it would be warm as well as grown up.

Even the romantic scene I was reading in *Wieland* could not keep my interest as I kept jumping up to see if Seth was coming. Finally I heard his footsteps in the dooryard, and the door opened.

"Happy birth day, Seth," Widow Chase and I said together, as we had planned.

"You are five years old now." I pointed to the garments and the cakes on the table.

Seth looked from me to the table to Widow Chase and then back again. "For me?"

"For you."

He reached immediately for one of the cakes.

"Here, now, try on your new clothes." Widow Chase picked up the waistcoat and helped Seth put his arm, cake and all, into the sleeve. The waistcoat fit beautifully. "I made you the waistcoat, and your sister sewed the coat."

"You already made me new shirts. And stockings. And bought shoes." Seth looked overwhelmed.

"Do you like them?" It was clear he did, but I wanted to hear the words.

"Yes, Abbie. Thank you. Thank you very much!" He flung himself on me, and then turned and did the same to Widow Chase. "And the cakes are for me, too? Just for me?"

"Just for you. But save some room for the chowder for supper."

Seth's coat fit just fine, too. I was very proud to have made it for him and to have helped plan such a special day. He took off the coat, as it was too warm, but he left the waistcoat on until it was time for sleep.

After supper he sat quietly on the bench, careful not to rumple his new clothes, when he suddenly noticed something.

"There is a ship on my waistcoat!" The small silk embroidery on the bottom front of the waistcoat was in black silk, and on the black wool it was a subtle design.

"I thought a future mariner would like a ship to remind him of his future," said Widow Chase.

"It is a beautiful ship. I wish Pa were here to see it. I would share my cakes with him."

"Seth, you've had a wonderful birth day." I thought of Ma. I knew that such a wonderful day would not have happened if she were still alive. I loved her so very much, but I couldn't help being glad we were now with Widow Chase. "Just forget about Pa! He isn't here and he never remembered your birth day in any case. He wasn't even home the day you were born!"

"He loves me, Abbie. He does. He told me he always wanted a son. He said the day he heard about me was the proudest day of his life!" Seth stood with his hands clenched. "Don't you say bad things about Pa!"

"Seth, I'm sorry. But we were having such a happy day. Let's just enjoy the day."

"Pa will be home. He will be home soon. I know it."

Seth was restless with dreams, or perhaps with too many cakes, all the night, and I had trouble sleeping, too.

The next night a knocking at the front door startled us all.

The sun was already down, supper was finished, and the candle lit. We had spent Saturday slicing early apples and stringing the pieces on long threads to dry in the attic for winter pies. It had been a long day, and the kitchen and our hands still smelled of the sweetness of the apples. Now we were sitting quietly by the kitchen fire. Widow

Chase was reading a Bible story to Seth while I knit a new black shawl for myself. She bade us sit where we were, and lit another candle to take with her as she went to see who would be calling so late in the day.

I heard Mr. Bowman's voice. Then the parlor door closed. It was most unusual for Mr. Bowman to call after supper without our expecting him. I waited a few minutes before I picked up the Bible and continued reading the story of Jonah to Seth.

"Did Jonah really live inside the whale, Abbie?"

"The Bible says so."

"When fishermen sail deep waters, they see whales. Sometimes they kill them."

"That is true."

"When they open them up, have they ever found a man alive?"

"Not that I have heard, Seth. But there are many things I have not heard of. And perhaps whales were different in Bible times."

"Maybe whales were as big as this house. As big as the church. As big as a moose!"

"Maybe, Seth."

I heard the front door closing; Mr. Bowman must have left.

Widow Chase joined us in a few minutes. She did not smile or look at us directly.

"Widow Chase, is a whale as big as a moose?"

"Bigger, Seth. Some whales are bigger than a whole moose family."

Seth thought about that for a moment. We were all quiet, looking at the fire, and into our own thoughts.

Something was wrong. I wondered if Mr. Bowman had come to tell Widow Chase she had even less money than she knew, or if something had happened to Mrs. Bowman. Even when she was not well Widow Chase was not usually far from the beginning of a smile. She looked very far from one now.

"Abbie and Seth, I have something to tell you." Her voice was low and firm.

I put the Bible down on the table.

"Mr. Bowman has just been here to deliver some news. News that, I fear, is not happy." It was difficult for her to tell whatever she had heard. "One of Mr. Bowman's friends, Enoch Greenleaf, received a letter today from an acquaintance of his who lives on Barbados. It contained word of several Wiscasset men."

I was suddenly very cold. I knew what she would say before I heard it.

"Your pa, as you know, sailed on another vessel after he left the *Fame*. He, along with Eben Greenleaf, a cousin of Enoch's, signed on with the *Golden Eagle,* bound for Spain."

"Pa is in Spain?" Seth's face lit with hope. "Is Spain far from Wiscasset? Will he be home soon? Will he be able to see my new waistcoat with the ship on it?"

"No, Seth, your pa is not in Spain. Listen carefully. England and Spain are now at war."

"Yes. And the United States is neutral. We are not at war with either country." I was proud I had remembered. Widow Chase had been teaching me about events in the world. It was interesting, but I did not see how it affected us in Wiscasset.

"That's right, Abbie. But England needs more sailors for its navy. Sometimes it stops American ships and takes our sailors to serve in English ships."

"That's not fair!" said Seth.

"No, it is not," agreed Widow Chase. "But it happens, nevertheless. It is called 'impressing.' Many American mariners have been impressed and forced to serve in the English navy."

I remembered Louise Bowman talking about mariners being impressed by the English. "Is that what happened to our pa?"

"That is what almost happened to your pa, Abbie. The English did capture the *Golden Eagle,* but when they tried to impress your father, he fought back. He was hurt. He fell overboard."

"Pa can swim," said Seth. "If Pa fell overboard, he would swim."

"This time he could not swim." Widow Chase moved from her chair and sat next to Seth on the bench, putting her arm around him. "He was hurt, Seth, and the water was very deep and very cold. He could not swim." She looked at me, took a deep breath, and said the words we were all thinking. "He is dead, Seth. Your pa drowned."

A part of me deep inside was glad the long waiting was over. But I did not want to think about how pa had died. "And Eben Greenleaf and the rest of the men on the *Golden Eagle*?"

"After your pa drowned, no one else resisted. Eben Greenleaf and four other men were impressed into the English navy. The *Golden Eagle* continued its journey to Spain, and then back to Barbados, where the mariners on board told their story."

"Pa is not coming back?" Seth's voice was almost a whisper.

"No, Seth, Pa is not coming back." I answered him before the widow could. It was my story, too.

"Ever? Not ever coming back?"

Seeing Seth's eyes fill with tears was harder than knowing about Pa.

"Not ever, Seth." My voice caught in my throat. "Not ever. Like Ma."

Seth buried his head in Widow Chase's arms. She rocked him silently, the way she would soon rock her own child.

Seth suddenly sat up. The tears on his face were shiny in the firelight. "I never got to show him my waistcoat or my new shoes! It isn't fair! I have new clothes and I am five years old and I am learning to read and I can't tell Pa!"

"You can pray to him, Seth. He is in Heaven now and he will hear you."

Seth buried his head in Widow Chase's arms again. "Praying isn't the same as talking," Seth sobbed. "Not the same at all."

"No, Seth, it is not. But sometimes it is all we can do." Widow Chase was crying now, too. "Sometimes life isn't the way we plan or hope it will be."

I was numb and cold at the same time. I hadn't counted on Pa's returning, but I hadn't wanted his death, either.

"Abbie, I am so very sorry." Widow Chase gestured that I, too, was welcome to share the bench and an embrace.

I didn't want her comfort. I wanted Ma back. I wanted life the way it used to be. I stayed in my chair. "He had been gone a long time," I answered. "He had not been our pa for a long time."

The candle burned down, and the room faded into the night.

Louisa Bowman had been right. Seth and I were orphans. Now there was no doubt. We could count on no one to care about us but ourselves. I knew we had not been able to depend on Pa for a long time. But he had always been a part of our lives and now he was gone. We were free to move on. But move on to where? What if Widow Chase left? What could I do to take care of Seth and keep us together?

Ma's eider duck was barely visible in the shadows of the candlelight. The life we shared with her, and with Pa, was gone forever.

Chapter 9

October 1806

Seth's nightmares returned. He found it hard to sleep and harder still to rise in the dark October mornings. And I found it harder and harder to be patient with him.

"I don't want to get up." Seth rolled over, covering his head.

"You have to get up. It is time for your chores and time for school."

"Don't want to go to school." Seth's voice was muffled under the pile of quilts. "Want to stay home with you."

"You have to learn to read and write. Seth, get up. Your breakfast is almost ready."

"You can teach me to read and write, Abbie. I don't have to go to school."

"You have to go to school." I pulled the bed coverings off Seth as he tried to burrow further into the pallet. "I know you did not sleep well. How could I not know? Between the northwest wind blowing the rain against the house and you kicking and moaning half the night, no one could sleep well. But now it is morning. I am going to pour a dipper full of cold water on your head if you do not get up right now."

Seth glared at me. He got up and headed toward the pump and the privy in the backyard. His first chore was to get washed up and bring in a load of firewood.

I straightened our pallet. It was right that a boy should miss his father. But it had been over a year since Seth had seen Pa. It was time for him to get on with life. We had to focus on our future, not our past. There must be something we could do to make our future more certain. Nothing could be done about the past. Life had to be dealt with. You couldn't spend your days under the quilts, much as you might want to.

Seth burst back into the kitchen, his face red with scrubbing, his eyes still swollen from last night's crying. He dropped four damp logs on the pile next to the fireplace. "Did you make apple pie for breakfast, Abbie? I could eat one hundred apple pies!"

I put one piece in front of him with a slice of ham and some beans. "You and your stomach woke up quick enough. You had better start with one piece of pie. I've already had mine. I will ask Widow Chase whether she needs anything before we leave." Widow Chase was more tired these days. She often stayed to her bed until after I left to walk Seth to school. I had more to do each day, as she rested.

"Abbie, I am five years old now. I can walk to school by myself. None of the big boys walk to school with their sisters." Seth chewed loudly.

It was true. The other boys walked alone or with each other. But Seth had never wanted to do so. To the contrary, since hearing of Pa's death he had clung to me even more than usual.

"Are you sure, Seth? I do not mind the walk."

"I am sure. I don't need anyone to walk with me. And you have to take care of Widow Chase all the time. If I walk alone you don't have to waste time with me."

I hesitated. Seth was five years old, but only yesterday he had begged me not to leave him at the school door. Ten minutes before he had not even wanted to get out of bed.

"I am going to be a blue-water mariner. Mariners do not have to walk to school with their sisters."

Maybe this was a step toward growing up. I certainly could not walk Seth to school for the rest of his life. And I could use the extra time to get the day's work started. "All right, then. Just don't dawdle or spend too much time kicking piles of red and yellow leaves and not enough time walking. Your teacher won't want you to be late."

He stuffed the last of the apple pie in his mouth and grabbed the dinner pail I had already filled for him. "I am not a little boy anymore, Abbie. I am going to be a mariner. I have to plan for the future, like you. I know what I have to do."

"You have to learn to read and write. I know. Just be careful. Go straight to school and come straight home." I hugged him.

Seth pulled out of my embrace and ran for the door. It was hard to think he was the same boy who had cried in his sleep half the night before.

It was a normal October day. Clouds were dark and low after last night's rain, and the damp air offered no reason to leave the house to go farther than the woodpile. I cooked, cleaned, and sewed some, and read with Widow Chase as she embroidered cradle hangings. Both of us were quiet. It did not seem a day for idle chatter.

I thought of Seth often. I had missed the walk to school, his hand in mine. But how proud he would be when he returned home, knowing he had walked to and from school by himself. Maybe being a little more independent was a way he could deal with losing Pa. It had not been an easy month for either of us. I wished I were five years old, knowing only that my duty was to go to school, and that there would be supper waiting when I returned. Life was so much more complicated now.

I expected Seth home by two. He had not returned by half past the hour.

"He has probably found some other boys to play with or a squirrel to chase. He must be feeling very grown up." Widow Chase smiled. "Abbie, you don't need to pace the room and keep looking out the windows. He will be home soon."

By three o'clock we were both worried.

"Start walking toward the school. You do not want to embarrass him. But he should have been home by now. It will be dark in little over an hour."

I threw on my cloak and headed toward the road Seth would have taken to school. The streets were filled with wet fallen leaves. Dark clouds hung low over the church steeple.

Two of the Nichols boys were playing ball in front of their home. "Hey, Abbie," Samuel called out. "Is Seth sick?"

"Sick?"

"He wasn't in school today. Teacher thought he must be sick, since you didn't bring him." He threw the ball to his brother.

"Are you certain he wasn't in school?"

Samuel looked at me askance. The school was one room, and Samuel was Seth's best friend. Of course he would be certain. "And he wasn't anywhere on the road to the school. I know because I stayed to help clean up. I just got back here."

"Thank you, Samuel. If you see Seth, will you tell him to get right home?"

"I will." He looked at me curiously before returning to his game.

I started toward the school. But—no. Samuel had said Seth wasn't there. I thought of going home. But Widow Chase was there and she would be looking out for Seth. I could not think what to do. Seth had run away before, but never had he been gone for so long.

How could I have let him go off alone? He was only five years old. Anything could have happened to him.

I thought of Ma and of Pa. There were just Seth and me now. Nothing could happen to Seth. It just couldn't.

But it had been hours since Seth had left for school. Where could he have gone?

I forced myself to concentrate. Where did Seth go other times when he ran away?

I headed toward the docks. My feet slipped on damp leaves as I ran down Main Street toward the river.

The wharves were never empty, but summer's activity had slowed and the dank day did not encourage anyone to loiter. I stopped everyone I saw.

"Please, have you seen Seth Chambers?"

Widow Wink hadn't seen him in a week. Mr. Dole just shook his head. Mr. Tucker asked his son, Jason. No one remembered seeing him.

I stood near Payson's Wharf. It was beginning to rain again. Drops of water fell from my hair down my face. I looked at the dark gray of the deep river. Pa had been one of the few mariners in Wiscasset who could swim, and he had taught Seth. But Pa had drowned.

Seth must be all right. He must. I brushed the tears and rain from my face and continued down Water Street, past Johnston's Wharf and shipyard. Wood's Wharf was the last one, around the bend, on Front

Street. Two cod fishermen were there, probably preparing their vessel to make a last fall run to the Grand Banks, off Nova Scotia, in Canada. I didn't know them; fishermen were at sea much of the time, and many lived downriver in harbor towns nearer the ocean, or on islands, like Monhegan or Damariscove. But the look—and smell—of their boat was unmistakable.

"Have either of you seen a young boy named Seth? About this tall"—I indicated my chest—"with curly red hair." I hoped the rain hid my tears. "He's been gone since morning."

"Sounds like the boy who was with Noah earlier, doesn't it?" the taller of the two asked the other. His broad shoulders and weathered face were clearly those of a man who had spent his life at sea pulling thousands of lines from deep waters.

His companion nodded. "It does. Is the boy you're looking for dressed in mourning?"

"Yes. Yes, he is. Where is he, please? When did you see him?"

"He and Noah Brown were here this morning. The boy helped Noah stow his gear on board the *Emma,* here. He was begging us to let him sail with Noah, but we told him to wait a few years. Haven't seen them since. But Noah should be back soon. We're sailing within the hour. Spending the night on Damariscove. We pick up two men there."

Noah would have taken care of Seth. Maybe he was all right. "Where is Noah? Do you know where he is staying?"

"Been boarding at Mrs. Nordstrom's, so far as I know," said the tall man.

I started running, calling out my thanks as I went. Seth must be with Noah. He must be with Noah. The sound of my pounding feet echoed my thoughts. He must be with Noah.

I knew Mrs. Nordstrom. She was the midwife Ma had with her when Seth was born. The one Widow Chase would call soon. She lived at the far end of Water Street. I ran past Johnston's Wharf. General Wood's Wharf. Payson's Wharf. Union Wharf. Carlton's Wharf, where a crowd had gathered around a coaster about to leave for Boston. Dole's Wharf. And then, where the river was mud at lowest tides, Cook's Wharf. Mrs. Nordstrom's house was just beyond.

I knocked on the door and leaned against it, trying to get my breath. My side hurt, and my feet. Please, please, I prayed silently. Please let Seth be here with

Noah. Let him be safe. Please. He's the only brother I have. He's all I have left.

I almost fell as the door opened. Mrs. Nordstrom recognized me. "Abbie. Come in, girl."

I stepped into her hallway, my cloak and hair dripping water on the wide, scrubbed pine boards; my feet muddy. "Please, Mrs. Nordstrom." I saw the tracks I had made and started to step back out into the street.

"Never you mind about the floor. It's Seth, isn't it?"

"Yes, ma'am."

"Well, you've found him, then. He's upstairs with Noah. I wondered when you'd be coming. He's been here and about all day."

"Then—he's all right?"

"Right as rain, girl. And drier than you, I trust. You just go on upstairs and knock. Second door to the left."

I went up the steep steps to the second-floor landing. There was but one small window in the hallway, and outside it was almost night. I felt along the hallway until I found the second door on the left and knocked.

Noah opened it.

The room was small and low, with a dormer that kept Noah from being able to stand up straight. I looked behind him. Seth was sitting on one of four pallets on the floor. There was nothing else in the room but Seth's dinner pail.

"Abbie!" Seth said.

"Seth Chambers. Where have you been? Have you any idea of how I worried? Have you any idea of what I was thinking?" I went straight past Noah over to Seth, dropping down next to him on the pallet and holding him tight. "What would I have done if you had disappeared?" I pulled back to look at him.

He had been crying.

"Are you hurt? Seth, are you all right?"

"He's fine, Miss Abbie," Noah answered. "He's just feeling a little sad."

"I wanted to be a mariner, Abbie. I wanted to be like Pa. I wanted Noah to take me with him to sea. But Noah's leaving. He's leaving tonight. And he's not coming back. Not ever." Seth's tears overflowed again. "Just like Pa."

I held Seth close and looked at Noah.

"I've been trying to tell him," Noah said. "I can't stay. People like me, we need to be in Canada, where no man can own another man."

I knew some people who had dark skin like Noah lived in Maine. They didn't have to go to Canada. "But there is no slavery here. Not since before I was born."

"True, miss. But I come from down south some, in Charleston, where I was a slave. There's a law says someone could claim a reward for taking me back there."

"But Charleston is so far!"

"I thought it was. I thought the District of Maine would be a safe place. But it's not far enough. Not by ship, it isn't. Not nearly far enough."

"You're going to Canada?"

"Amos Brewer, he's going to let me work on his fishing boat for my fare. He'll take me to a place called Lunenburg. Folks say jobs are there for a man who knows ships. A man like me can make a living there. And be free."

"A man needs to be free," I agreed, and looked at Seth. "Noah has to go. He has no choice."

Seth sobbed. "I know. He said so. But it isn't fair. Ma died, and Pa died, and now Noah is going. It isn't fair."

"No. It is not fair, Seth," Noah said. "And I'm sorry to leave you. But it has to be done." He looked at me. "You understand, Miss Abbie? You'll help Seth to understand?"

I wish I understood better. It wasn't fair. Noah should be able to live anywhere he chose. "I'll try."

"But why can't you stay here? You like us. You like

Wiscasset. Why can't you stay here?" Seth hiccuped through his tears.

"Seth, I do like you. But everyone has to find his own right place. A place he can call home. Some people are lucky. They're born in their right place and can stay there. But, Carolina, where I was born, was not the right place for me. I like Wiscasset. Yours is a beautiful town, even on such a cold and rainy day as this one. But it is not the right place for me. There are people here who would do me harm. Would take me back to Charleston and claim a reward for doing so." He paused. "Some people have to look their whole life for a place. From what I've heard, this Lunenburg, in Canada, may be the home I've been looking for."

"Can I come visit you at your new home?"

"Sure, you can. When you're a little bigger, maybe you'll come up and fish the Grand Banks for cod, like Mr. Brewer." Noah looked out the window. "I need to be going now, Seth. They'll be waiting for me on the *Emma*."

Seth and I got up. We all went down the narrow stairway. Mrs. Nordstrom gave Noah a hug. "Be well, Noah. Get word back to us when you are safe."

"I will. As soon as I can."

"Don't you worry"—Mrs. Nordstrom touched his shoulder—"I'll pass word to Seth and Abbie, too."

"Thank you. For everything." Noah looked at all of us. "Wiscasset is a good place. Maybe someday there will be space for me in a town like this. But not now." He gave Seth one more hug. "Take care of your sister, Seth. Go back to school and learn to read and write. Grow up to be a good and fair man. Maybe I'll see you one day on the coast of Canada." He tipped his cap to us all. "Good-bye."

He headed down Water Street through the dark. Seth moved to follow Noah, and I reached for his hand.

"Here, child." Mrs. Nordstrom handed me a pierced tin lantern holding a lit candle. "This will help you see your way home. Widow Chase will be worrying over you."

"Thank you. I'll return the lantern tomorrow." Seth was still sniffling and looking down the way Noah had gone.

"When you can. Now, both of you, go on and get home."

We stepped out onto Water Street, still holding hands, and walked through the darkness and light rain toward the center of town.

"Noah is a good man, isn't he, Abbie?"

"Yes, Seth. Noah is a very good man."

"Someday I am going to visit him at his home in Canada. He said I could."

"That would be a good thing, Seth. That would be a very good thing. And in the meantime, you stay and help me."

"Help you? You don't need any help, Abbie. You spend all your time with Widow Chase."

"Widow Chase does need special help, Seth. She will for a time. But our helping her earns us a place to live; a place we can be together. I don't want you to go away, like Pa and Noah. I want you to stay here, and help in keeping wood on the fire, and sweeping the kitchen, and doing your schoolwork. I want you to stay here so we can be a family."

I stopped, right in the middle of Main Street, and gave him a hug. "You're the only family I've got, Seth Chambers, and I want you here with me, growing up to be a good man, like Noah said."

"All right, Abbie. I guess so. I want us to be a family."

We were almost to Union Street.

"Abbie, is supper ready? I'm hungry. I'm so hungry, I think I could eat a whole moose!"

"When was I to get supper when I've been chasing

all over town for you?" I raised the lantern higher as we got closer to Widow Chase's house. "But I think there's some apple pie and beef soup that could be heated."

Seth broke away from me and ran toward the door.

Chapter 10

November 1806

The gusts off the river were cold, and I was glad to have two pairs of long stockings under my skirts and petticoats to keep the winds off my legs. Walking tired Widow Chase as her time came closer. She was growing to depend on my doing errands for her. This day she had sent me to Mr. Johnston's store for white and black embroidery floss silk.

I pulled the ribbons on my new bonnet tighter and held my cloak close as I headed down Main Street. My hands were sore. Seth and I had spent the past two days, Saturday and again Sunday after church, interweaving pine and spruce boughs around the base of the house as high as the windows and filling in the spaces with hay. Boughs surrounded most homes in

Wiscasset at this time of year. Such work had been done by the Abenakis before the colonists and surely helped to keep winter winds from finding their way through pine clapboards. But today my hands were cut and scratched from the rough branches, and my shoulders ached from the heavy work. I was glad the task was complete for the winter. In past years Widow Wink's brother had done such chores for the house we had lived in, and Captain Chase or his crew had prepared his house for winter. This year it was up to Seth and me.

A hard frost last night had covered rocks at the high tide mark with thin ice. Small black and white bufflehead ducks were on the river, and an occasional eider, blown in from the sea. I shivered. As yet no heavy snow had fallen, but winter was surely upon us.

Warmth welcomed me as I opened the door to Mr. Johnston's store. I held my hands toward the fireplace, as I could see Mr. Johnston was occupied. Three finely dressed ladies whom I did not recognize were claiming his attention. No doubt they had more money in their pockets to spend for his time and goods than did I.

I did not look directly at them, as that would not have been polite. But I glanced often, curious to see their style of dress. Since Widow Chase had introduced me to various fashions I had become quite conscious of women's clothing. The older woman, apparently the mother, was elegantly dressed in the style of a year or two ago, which was still much favored by many: a wide-skirted, open gown with a square neckline and long, tight sleeves. The green fabric was shiny. I wondered if it was lustring, a silk I had recently heard Widow Chase speak of. The woman also wore a long cloak of what I believed to be beaver fur.

The two younger women, who looked about the ages of Widow Chase and Mrs. Bowman, wore loose French empire-style gowns with high waists and sleeves puffed at the shoulders and tight at the wrists. The taller woman's gown was blue silk; the other's, yellow. Both women wore cloaks of embroidered velvet, trimmed with the same fur as their mother's cape. I knew of no one in Wiscasset, save perhaps General Wood's wife, who dressed so elegantly.

I pulled my own black wool cloak, which pleased and warmed me well, around my muslin bodice and skirts.

"You have nothing, then, to show us?" The older woman was not pleased.

"I am sorry, Mrs. Lenox, but you are now in the

District of Maine, not in Philadelphia. Here most women make their own gowns and hats and such. Or order them from Boston."

"I am very aware, sir, of what part of this land I am in." Mrs. Lenox looked disdainfully at Mr. Johnston. "This store's provisions alone show just how far we have traveled in the past week."

Her daughters giggled a bit behind their fingers. Despite all their finery they acted like little girls in a schoolyard.

"Mrs. Lenox, I do carry a wide assortment of fine silks and ribbons. May I show you . . ." Mr. Johnston gestured toward the bolts of fabrics that filled the shelves in back of his counter.

"We do not have the time. We need new hats for Thanksgiving. We never thought Wiscasset would be so far from civilization that it would not even contain one millinery shop. We have no time to order from Boston. Surely you have some woman in town who can work with straws and velvets and who knows current fashion?"

As she spoke, I moved closer to them. My own hat, which Widow Chase had fashioned, was, indeed, though in the black of mourning, of both straw and velvet. I had copied the form from one of the newspaper drawings we had obtained and Widow Chase had embellished it well, although not as elaborately as she would have a grown woman's headpiece.

"Please, madam, perhaps I could be of service." My heart was pounding, but I could not contain my thoughts. Nor my tongue. I untied my hat and held it out to her. "I work for a woman who does well with both straws and velvets. She fashioned this bonnet. She is also accomplished at embroideries and ruffles and ribbons. I am sure she could make you the head-wear you desire."

Mr. Johnston stared at me. Then he smiled, very slightly. I did not know whether he was laughing at me for my audacity or if he was amused by my daring. I myself could hardly believe my words.

Mrs. Lenox took my hat, turning it this way and that. "It is well crafted, although of a simpler style than I had in mind." She turned to show it to her daughters. "And the shape is quite stylish." She handed my hat back to me. "This woman you work for—she is a milliner?"

I took a deep breath. "Recently so, Mrs. Lenox." I ignored Mr. Johnston, who was shaking his head slightly. "So recently as for Mr. Johnston to be unaware of her services."

"Has she a shop nearby?"

"No," I said quickly. "Not as yet. She works at her home. But she would be happy to visit you at the place you are staying, and there learn what manner of head coverings you would want, and in what colors and designs."

"And could such head coverings be completed by Thanksgiving?"

Thanksgiving was in ten days. Surely Widow Chase could do that. "Yes, certainly. If the designs and fabrics were determined soon."

"We are staying with Captain William Nichols and his wife, my cousin Jane, in their home two blocks north of here on Main Street." She turned to Mr. Johnston. "Of course, they will soon be moving the house, and building a home more appropriate to their station and family size. But, for now, the home is—cozy." She looked at me. "Do you know the home of Captain Nichols?"

"Yes, ma'am." It was next to the public water pump at the corner of Main and Federal Streets, not far from the Chase house.

"Then have your mistress come to see me there at two this afternoon and we shall see whether she is capable of creating what we need."

"I will," I agreed, and the three women moved toward the door.

"I cannot believe there is not a single millinery shop in town. At least one woman is smart enough to recognize a need and try to fill it."

The shop door closed with a bang.

"So Widow Chase is now a milliner?" Mr. Johnston laughed and shook his head. "Abbie, I wouldn't want to be you when you get back to her this morning." He turned to put some fabric back on the shelf. "A lady like Widow Chase? Take in millinery work? Not likely."

"Mr. Johnston, I came to buy some floss silk."

"Certainly, Abbie." He was still smiling as he reached under the counter for the drawer of floss. "Colors?"

"Only black and white today." I wondered what colors the ladies would be wanting on their bonnets. Widow Chase had the best hands for making hats in Wiscasset, of that I was sure. She made hats for herself and for Mrs. Bowman, and now even for me. And she needed an income—that I knew well enough.

I exchanged my coins for the floss.

She would think me brash and impudent. But sometimes you have to speak up and take advantage of an opportunity. If only Widow Chase would see Mrs. Lenox and her daughters as an opportunity.

She was hemming clouts for the baby when I reached home. "Were you able to get the floss?"

"Yes, Widow Chase." I hung up my cloak and bonnet and put the floss on the table.

I did not know how best to begin. On my walk home I had seen clearly how I had overstepped my place and might well have put Widow Chase in an embarrassing position. She knew Mrs. Nichols; how could she go to her home as a paid laborer?

I stood silently, unable to think of the right words.

"Yes, Abbie? You look as if you have something on your mind."

"Widow Chase, I am so very sorry, but it seemed the right thing to do at the time and I know I shouldn't have, but I did, and you may hate me forever, but I meant it to be a help." The words spilled out.

"Abbie, slow down. Now come over and sit." She patted a place on the bench next to her chair. "Now, what is it that I shall hate you for?"

"I told her you were a milliner!"

"You what?" Widow Chase dropped her sewing on her lap. "You told what, and to whom?"

"There was a woman—three women, really—at

Mr. Johnston's store and they were looking for hats, and Mr. Johnston said he had none, and I showed them the bonnet that you made for me, and they liked it and I said you could make hats for them, for Thanksgiving. And I told them you were a milliner, and they are expecting you to call at Captain Nichols's home at two this afternoon, and I am very sorry, but you make such beautiful hats, and they looked as though they would pay well, and I just spoke without thinking." I took a deep breath.

Widow Chase spoke slowly and softly. "You told these three women I would make hats for them?"

"By Thanksgiving."

"And they believe I am a milliner?"

I nodded.

"Because you told them that?"

"Yes." I looked down at the floor for a moment, and then at her again. "You do make the most beautiful hats in Wiscasset, Widow Chase, and you said you had to find a way to have more income, and . . ."

She just sat quietly.

"I didn't mean for you to be embarrassed. I spoke too quickly, without thinking. I can go and tell them it is impossible." I jumped up and grabbed my cloak off the hook. "I can go right now."

"Wait! Abbie, stop," Widow Chase said. "How were these women dressed?"

"In fashion. They were an older woman and her two daughters, from Philadelphia. The older woman, Mrs. Lenox, was dressed in a full gown and bodice, and her daughters were in empire silk dresses patterned as the ones you have shown me in the newspapers." I hung up my cloak again. "The daughters wore embroidered capes trimmed with fur, and Mrs. Lenox wore a fur cape."

"What style hat or bonnet do you think would be their choice?"

"They liked the shape of mine. They would want the latest styles."

"You just walked up to them and showed them your bonnet?" Widow Chase was smiling now.

"Yes."

"Abbie, you are an amazing girl. There is no way in the world I would have had the courage to do that. And yet, perhaps you are right. Perhaps you have found a solution to our problems."

"Mr. Johnston said you were a lady and would not work for others." I thought of Widow Wink and her ginger beer. And Mrs. Light, who sold eggs. And Mrs. Anderson, who made and sold peppermints and molasses candy. They were not so elegant or so young as Widow Chase, but they were respected in Wiscasset, so far as I knew.

"A woman can be a lady and still earn a living." She hesitated. "At least I think she can. Although I suspect my mother would agree with Mr. Johnston." She put the clouts in a basket next to her chair and brushed some threads off her skirt. "When am I to be at the Nicholses' home to meet these women?"

"At two o'clock this afternoon."

"Then I had better dress in my best gown and hat." She rose.

"You will go?"

"I will go, Abbie." She reached out to give me a hug, which was difficult since she was so big with the baby. "We may both be crazy, but I will go."

She looked down at her belly and patted it. "Baby, did you know your mother was a milliner? Abbie, if this works, you will be my assistant. I will need your help with forming the straw. For now, you will get dinner on the table while I choose proper attire." She headed for her bedchamber. "In mourning and near confinement. If I can find anything appropriate to wear today, then I should always be able to do so."

I sat down. She did not hate me. She was going to see Mrs. Lenox. And she had said I might be her assistant. An assistant milliner.

I hugged myself and grinned. Life was full of wondrous possibilities indeed.

Chapter 11

Thanksgiving, 1806

"What about a turkey?" Seth looked at the kitchen table in dismay. It was covered with pieces of straw and silks and velvets and ribbons. "People have turkeys for Thanksgiving. And pumpkin pies. And puddings. And pickles! All we have are hats!"

"They have turkeys?" I teased him. "Are you sure they don't have hats?"

Seth made a face and stomped back to the pallet, where he had made a kind of cave with the quilts and blankets.

The days before Thanksgiving were long and very busy. I formed the straw as Widow Chase directed, and she did all of the trimming and ruffles. There was not much sleeping done, but the three hats for Mrs. Lenox and her daughters were completed ahead of the date they were promised.

"Can you believe it, Sally? They liked the hats so well, they each ordered another, to be completed before their ship sails south for Philadelphia." Widow Chase gestured around the kitchen, taking in the kitchen table covered with sewing supplies, the pile of straw on the floor near the door, and her overflowing bag of ribbons and trims and floss for embroidery. "Which has left us in the midst of a bit of chaos. But very happy."

"Lydia, this is the smartest step you have taken in months." Mrs. Bowman was visiting and had joined us in the kitchen. With hats to be finished there was no time for parlor sitting. I had served cups of tea without ceremony. Mrs. Bowman sipped hers while Widow Chase continued working at the table.

My straw work was also done in the kitchen, so the birch broom had to be used often, as pieces of thread and straw flew to all corners of the room. To save time for sewing I was cooking only simple breads and puddings and boiled dinners. But all was going well. The second group of hats was almost finished. Mrs. Lenox and her daughters were to sail for Philadelphia three days from now—two days after Thanksgiving.

"But can't we have a turkey?" Seth's head appeared

from under the quilts, and his plaintive voice filled the room. "Tomorrow is Thanksgiving. Everyone at school is going to have turkey for Thanksgiving!"

"We will have turkey, Seth," Widow Chase assured him. "We will take time off for turkey. I promise."

"You always had a talent for fancywork, Lydia, and a sense of style better than most in Wiscasset. And now you have Abbie"—Mrs. Bowman smiled at me as I kneaded the dough for Thanksgiving bread—"to help with the straw work and the stitching. Mr. Bowman and I are going to dinner at General Wood's home Friday night. I am going to tell all the ladies there what you have done. They have often admired my headgear. Now I will tell them plainly who did the work and that you would be pleased to do similar work for others. I know Mrs. Nichols admired your hats greatly when you brought them to her cousin. She told Mrs. Sewall, who mentioned it to Jonathan."

Widow Chase's fingers kept moving on the purple velvet bonnet trimmed with fur she was making for the youngest Miss Lenox. "It would be kind of you to mention me to the other women, Sally."

"They have money and they order hats and gowns from Boston and New York. I don't see why they wouldn't buy from you when you are right here in town. I will make sure to claim any newspapers Mr. Bowman has and bring them right to you, so you can see the styles being advertised. No one will be able to say your work is not of the times."

"That would be most helpful, Sally. I still cannot believe I am doing this, but if enough ladies are interested, then it is a solution to my problem."

"Our problem, Lydia. I could not have borne it if you had gone back to live in Augusta. I would have missed you so. And what would have happened to Abbie and Seth?"

I covered the dough with a cloth and put it on the hearth to warm so it would rise. I did not look up. There was no doubt that a millinery business for Widow Chase could well be the solution for all of us. But much as I wanted to believe all would be well, thinking so now would be counting chickens before they hatched. Or dollars, before they were in the bank.

"Abbie, can I have a piece of apple to eat?" Seth's whisper was louder than most people's voices. "Just a little piece of apple." He looked longingly at the bowl of dried apples I had left on the sideboard for pie.

"Give him a piece of apple, Abbie," Widow Chase said, laughing. "Otherwise he might starve before Thanksgiving. But just one piece, Seth. We need the rest for Thanksgiving pie." She shook her head at Mrs. Bowman and resumed her conversation as I got Seth his piece of apple. "I still have a little money left. With what I have earned for these six hats I should have enough to get us through my confinement and comfortably into the new year."

"Is all ready?" Mrs. Bowman asked. It was clear her friend's lying-in would be soon.

"Abbie and I have prepared all the necessary garments and blankets. I even found a cradle in the attic that must have been the captain's when he was a baby." It was a beautiful cradle, made of tiger maple. Widow Chase had made miniature wool hangings to cover it and keep out winter drafts. "Mrs. Nordstrom has agreed to be with me when called. She says it will be soon now."

"I hope you will also be calling me. You should not be alone at such a time, Lydia. Think of me as family." She looked toward me. "And of course Abbie will be here to help, also."

I thought of the betony I had prepared all those months ago. I had never been present at a birth, however, and I was glad Mrs. Bowman would be near, and Mrs. Nordstrom, who helped many Wiscasset women in their time. I had been only seven when Seth was born, and Ma had sent me to stay with Widow Wink until the birthing was over.

"Abbie can keep Seth out of the way."

"I am not in the way," Seth said as he pushed between me and the table to see what I was doing.

"Here, Seth; cut up the suet for the mincemeat." I handed him a knife. It was small, but adequate for the job. I watched him closely as I cut up the citrons and boiled beef that would also be part of the mincemeat. There was plenty to do. I then had to pound the cloves and allspice and cinnamon to add to the mixture.

Keeping Seth at a distance would not be easy, should the baby come when he was at home, but I would try. Widow Chase had a fireplace in her bedchamber and could give birth there. She had a door to close for privacy. For most women, like Ma, birthing in the kitchen near the fire was more likely.

As her time approached I had made sure ample wood was piled in Widow Chase's bedchamber. I had already washed clean sheets and cloths, in readiness. What more there was to do I did not know.

"I shall give you another millinery order right now, Lydia. I want you to make a special bonnet I can give to my mother as a gift for the New Year. A bright blue embroidered velvet, I think, because her eyes are blue."

"I would be happy to do so. As soon as I have finished these," Widow Chase gestured at the hats she was completing. "Next Monday, perhaps, you and I could go to see what colors Mr. Johnston has in stock and select the ones you like. But although I know New Year's is a time for gifts, I do not think I should take on other orders just now. Not until after my baby is born and I know all is well."

"Of course. I did not mean to ask too much of you," Mrs. Bowman replied. "You should only do what you feel you can. There will be plenty of time later." I was glad Widow Chase had such a friend. Mrs. Bowman continued. "I have been thinking that perhaps in January you could place a small advertisement for your business in the *Eastern Repository*. People here and elsewhere read that newspaper and would know to come to you when they were in town."

"Perhaps. I will think of that after the New Year."

"Lydia, I am just so excited for you! To be able to support yourself without depending on a husband! The prospect is delightful." She hesitated a moment. "Not that I am not very lucky to have Mr. Bowman to take care of such matters, of course." She patted her hair and started to get up. "I almost forgot to ask. You will let Jonathan and me drive you and Abbie and Seth to church from now on?"

"Thank you. That would be kind. The walk up the hill over the green is difficult now."

Mrs. Bowman picked up her cloak. "I will stop next Monday, and we will pick out the blue for my mother's hat. And"—she turned to include me—"we will be here with the sleigh or carriage on Sundays from now on."

I thanked Mrs. Bowman for including Seth and me, but I wondered whether Louisa would also be sharing that carriage. She often stayed with her grandparents on weekends and always sat with them in their pew. Mr. Bowman used to share the pew; now he and Mrs. Bowman had their own, as did Widow Chase, who shared hers with us. I did not think Louisa would be pleased to be seen sharing a carriage with a milliner and a hired girl. Even if the milliner was a lady.

"There is turkey. A fine turkey." Seth had not let me out of his sight since I rose early Thanksgiving morning to put the turkey on the large iron trammel, where it could hang and roast over the fire. I could easily turn and baste the bird as it cooked. Trammels that large were not common in Wiscasset. Ma had always managed to have boiled turkey with vegetables and pie on Thanksgiving. If Pa were with us we also had some nuts or sweets. Ma had loved Thanksgiving. But this Thanksgiving was a feast.

There was turkey with stuffing, a chicken pie, onions, turnips, cranberry sauce, cucumber pickles, and pickled peaches and pears, and then pies of mincemeat, pumpkin, and apple, and a plate of sage cheese to finish.

The kitchen table was still covered with ribbons, but Widow Chase had instructed me to set the table in the dining room. The three of us had dressed in our best and sat at the dark wood table together. I had laid a fire in the fireplace and polished the brass andirons and the silver candlesticks so they reflected the fire's warm glow.

Ma would have been amazed to see us sitting in this room, dressed as we were, choosing from such an assortment of dishes. Widow Chase had even given me a glass of her port wine. It was as sweet and delicious as I had suspected, and made the room seem even warmer and more welcoming.

The turkey was brown and crisp and delicious. Seth took another bite, and one of the onion and sage stuffing. "This is the best turkey in the world. The best turkey ever."

Seth was right.

It was the best turkey ever.

Chapter 12

Christmas Sunday, 1806

Christmas Sunday dawned cold and icy. It was snowing. It had snowed several hours each day for the past week. Windows rattled in the wind. Snowbanks were growing higher, bordering passageways to streets and woodpiles.

Seth could no longer help with the shoveling. The drifts were now above his head. Snow had first covered the pine boughs piled around the house and now covered the bottom half of the first-floor windows. The rooms were as dark as dusk all day long.

I pulled on three pairs of the heavy wool stockings I had knit, all my quilted petticoats and skirts, and covered myself with my cloak, which I fastened with pins as well as I could. I picked up the heavy wooden shovel.

In this weather, and with Widow Chase's situation, we needed to keep much dry wood available. The snow was not making that easy. Outside, tiny pieces of ice blew into my face and down the neck of my garments despite the hood on my cloak.

Although Mrs. Nordstrom had predicted in November that the baby could come at any time, it had not yet been born. "Sometimes first babies take their own time. All is fine," she had assured Widow Chase. It seemed we had been waiting for this baby forever.

I dug out the six inches of new snow that had fallen since nightfall on the path from the kitchen door to the privy and woodpile. The path would be filled with new snow sooner than I wanted to think. I then made a number of trips between the woodpile and the kitchen. The wood outside was frozen, one piece to another. The work was heavy and hard.

When the pile of wood inside appeared large enough for the day, I added logs to the fireplace, put on a kettle of snow to boil for tea water, since the pump outside had long since been frozen, and woke Seth.

"It is Sunday morning. We are to go with the Bowmans to Christmas services. Up with you, put on your coat, and wash your face in the snow. I will go to clear the front pathway."

The red brick walk from the front door to Union Street was also snowed in. I shoveled for longer than my shoulders would have liked. My fingers were numb before the passageway from the Chase house to the street was clear.

I was toasting some of yesterday's bread and cutting some slices of boiled beef for breakfast by the time the tea water was hot and Widow Chase had joined us in the kitchen. "A cold day," she said, rubbing the frost on a high pane of glass to try to see out. "How much more snow did we get last night?"

"Only six inches. But drifts filled the paths."

"I see you've been up early to get the wood." Her nod thanked me. "It will be a cold church service this morning." She warmed her hands by the fire as I put the teapot on the brick hearth so the tea would steep.

"Widow Chase, do you want me to get you some snow to wash your face?" Seth looked as though he had rolled in the snow rather than washed in it. His face was dry, but his coat and waistcoat were damp with melted snow.

"No, thank you," she replied, shaking her head at the sight of him. "I had some water in my basin upstairs. I was able to break the ice and wash by the fireplace."

Seth stood on the hearth, warming his hands and trying to dry his clothing.

"Seth, here. Have some toast and beef and blueberry pie." The sweetness of dried blueberries was welcome on a cold morning. "Eat well. It is Christmas Sunday. Services will be long today." The Reverend Packard's wife had given him a pine hourglass carved with ships and filled with sea sand to put on his pulpit to remind him when his sermons ran longer than one hour, but often he forgot to look at it.

"Christmas is when the baby Jesus was born."

"That's right, Seth. Now, eat up."

Every year the Reverend Packard preached a special sermon on the Sunday closest to Christmas. Today was that day. Christmas day was not a holiday for Congregationalists to celebrate except in church. Ma had told me that in Baltimore and parts of the south, Christmas was a time for parties and fireworks. In Wiscasset it was a time for prayer.

We had hardly finished breakfast when a knocking on the door meant the Bowmans had arrived.

"We will clean up later," Widow Chase confirmed. "Seth, take a quilt from your pallet to cover you and Abbie at church." She tried to help him, but she could not reach so far. I quickly folded the quilt and handed it to Seth.

"I've already brought down a quilt for my use," said Widow Chase. "It is in the front hall."

Seth ran toward the front door.

The path I had dug was now covered by a new inch of snow, but Mr. Bowman had kindly cut two steps in the end of the snowbank near the road so we could easily get up to his sleigh. Enough sleighs had passed to pack the snow down, and although the poor, cold horses were stamping their hooves and breathing heavily, I was glad of the ride.

Mr. Bowman helped Widow Chase up next to Mrs. Bowman, and then lifted Seth. I scrambled on myself. The fit in the sleigh was tight, but there was room for all of us when Seth sat on my lap. I was relieved to see Louisa was not there. She must be going to church with her grandparents today.

Services were long, as expected. We sat in the Chase pew, near the left front of the church. The sides of the pew kept drafts out but they also prevented Seth from seeing the rest of the congregation. Much of my time was spent in keeping him quiet rather than in concentrating on the Reverend Packard's words.

Widow Chase sat in her usual place in the corner

of the pew. Today she left concerns about Seth's rest-lessness to me. After the reverend had been preaching for some time, she closed her eyes. I hoped no one could see that she might have fallen asleep. Certainly she would not have been the first person in the Reverend Packard's congregation to fall asleep during a sermon, but I knew she would be embarrassed should anyone notice. And we were close to the front of the church, so the reverend himself might see. I was about to touch her, to waken her, when she sat up straight.

She whispered, "Abbie, I think we had better leave."

Whispering in church was strongly frowned upon. I looked quickly to see if anyone had heard. Perhaps Widow Chase did not realize she had only been asleep for a few moments. "The sermon is not yet ended. It is not time to go."

"It is time to go." She put her hand on top of where the baby was growing. "I'm certain it is time to go. The Reverend Packard must excuse us."

I jumped up, knocking the quilt off her lap. I tried to pick it up, as well as the one Seth and I were using, and to grab Seth. There was no way I could do all that and not be the object of attention. People all over the church were looking at us. I blushed with embarrassment.

To my great relief, Mrs. Bowman immediately left her own pew to join us. "Is it time?"

I nodded. "Widow Chase has to get home."

The Reverend Packard stopped his sermon. "Do you need assistance, Widow Chase?" his voice came loud, like the voice of God, from the pulpit.

"No, thank you, Reverend Packard. But I would ask that Mr. and Mrs. Bowman be excused from services to see me home." Widow Chase's voice rose as strong as the reverend's, despite her circumstances.

"Of course. You also take our prayers and best wishes home with you. A baby born on Christmas Sunday is surely a special blessing."

We made our way out of the church. Mr. Bowman took the blankets off his horses and brought his sleigh as close to the church door as possible. Mrs. Bowman and I supported Widow Chase. I held on to Seth with my other hand.

"It is still snowing!" He chattered, "This afternoon I will dig a tunnel from our path and build a secret house for me. I will make snowballs and throw them at tree branches so snow will fall down. I will—"

"Shush, Seth. There are more important events in life than building snow tunnels." I could hardly believe that the day had finally come for the baby to be born. And, for all my planning, I had never thought we would be in church when Widow Chase knew it was time.

Seth stuck his tongue out at me, and I pretended not to see. He did not question why we were leaving church before anyone else, and I did not bother to explain. He would know soon enough, and have questions enough. This was a time for Widow Chase, not for Seth.

The ride home was swift, despite the snow, although I could tell it was difficult for Widow Chase. Her face was white. She held very tightly to my hand and leaned heavily against Mrs. Bowman. Together we were able to get her into the house and up to her bedstead. Mr. Bowman went in search of Mrs. Nordstrom. I hoped she was stopping to home this day. I had not seen her at services.

Mrs. Bowman helped Widow Chase into bed while I went downstairs and began bringing more loads of wood up from the kitchen. We had already moved the widow's bedstead closer to the fireplace in anticipation of this day, although one couldn't move it too close for fear the bed hangings might catch fire. Without bed hangings, a bedstead would be cold indeed in winter, no matter the number of quilts available.

"I want to help! I can carry wood, too." Seth followed me so closely, he trod on my skirts and I almost fell.

"Just keep out of my way," I answered.

Seth could help a little, but most of the logs were too heavy for him, and I did not want him in the widow's chamber in any case.

"What is happening, Abbie? Is the baby going to come now? When is it going to come? Can I see it?"

"Seth, I am busy. Widow Chase and Mrs. Bowman need all my help just now. Let me take the wood upstairs. You bring some kindling and leave it next to her door."

"Why can't I go in her room? You can go in. Widow Chase likes me. Why won't she let me go in?"

"Seth, just shush. This is not a time for a child to be with Widow Chase. You can see her later, after the baby is born. For right now, just stay out of our way."

Seth pouted, but I didn't have time to deal with him. He did bring some small branches to her bedchamber door, and that was helpful.

I was much relieved when, after almost an hour, Mr. Bowman returned with Mrs. Nordstrom. She had been visiting her cousin on the opposite end of Water

Street, and he had to seek her out. She asked me to boil up water, and nodded approval as she looked over the pile of clean cloths and bedclothes I had prepared.

"Just keep the fire high, Abbie, and be nearby if we should need something. Don't be worrying about Widow Chase; she is young and healthy and will have a fine baby."

Widow Chase was making no noise, but she was holding tight to the bedposts, and I could see she was struggling not to cry out.

"You're old enough to see," said Mrs. Nordstrom. "No baby comes into the world without pain. Says so in the Bible. You go and melt as much snow as you can, boil it up, and then bring it upstairs and boil up some more."

"Yes, Mrs. Nordstrom." I wanted to be of help. And clearly I could be of more help heating snow and bringing firewood then I could be helping with the birth.

Mr. Bowman was in the kitchen when I got there, playing a finger shadow game with Seth. "Thank you," I said to him. It was a great relief not to have to worry about Seth for a few moments.

"How does it go?"

"More quickly, I think, than I have heard happens

with some women. Mrs. Nordstrom has asked that I heat snow and bring the boiled water upstairs."

"Let me help." Mr. Bowman looked elegant in his Sunday coat and breeches and yellow embroidered waistcoat, but I did not turn down his offer. He took the bucket and shovel and made several trips to the backyard, filling every bucket and pot and bowl I could find. I carefully filled the largest iron pot we had and set it on the crane, moving the other containers as close to the hearth as they would fit.

"I can help, too!" said Seth. He ran out the back door. As the snow melted in the warm kitchen we re-filled the containers. Since a great deal of snow melts to a small amount of water, Mr. Bowman and Seth made many trips to the yard while I kept pouring the water into the kettle. When it boiled, I carried it upstairs. Mr. Bowman kindly kept an eye on Seth, who seemed to think our goal was to bring every flake of snow from the yard into the kitchen. He did his best to do so.

Upstairs, Widow Chase was clearly in much dis-comfort. Mrs. Bowman was wiping her forehead, and Mrs. Nordstrom kept telling her to take deep breaths and not be afraid. I tried not to disturb anyone as I built the fire up a bit and left hot water on the shallow bedchamber hearth. I wondered what it would be like to have a baby. It was clear the suffering was terrible.

"She's doing fine, Abbie," Mrs. Nordstrom said. "And that betony she told me you prepared . . . that's helping, too. Don't worry, girl. Just keep bringing the hot water every ten minutes or so. It cools fast."

"Yes, Mrs. Nordstrom." I ran downstairs again, glad to do something to help.

The kitchen was cold, from all the trips outside, and Mr. Bowman and Seth were wet from the snow and the melted water. Even in the kitchen we could now hear moans from the bedchamber.

"Is Widow Chase having her baby right now?" Seth asked.

"Very soon, Seth." I pushed him gently out of my way as I reached into the fireplace to take the iron kettle of water off the crane.

"Is it a boy baby or a girl baby?"

"We don't know yet."

"Is Widow Chase very angry at the baby?"

"No, Seth." His questions never seemed to stop. "Why would you think such a thing?"

"Because she is yelling at the baby. I can hear her."

Mr. Bowman answered Seth this time. "Seth, Widow

Chase is not angry at the baby. She just doesn't feel very well now. Why don't you and I go and make that tunnel you talked about when we were leaving the church?"

"Thank you, Mr. Bowman." My relief was clear.

"But we will be close by, should you should need more snow or . . . if there is news . . . you will be sure to call us."

"Yes, sir. The very minute."

After that I took a number of pots of water to the bedroom, returning with the cool water to reheat it or get fresh, depending on whether it was used. It was getting late in the day. I was replacing the kettle on the crane, thinking Mr. Bowman and Seth should come in and have some tea because of the cold, when I heard the baby cry.

It was the most beautiful sound I had ever heard.

I ran to the kitchen door and called out, "Seth! Mr. Bowman! The baby! It has come!"

Mr. Bowman was at the side of the house, having dug an impressive tunnel almost halfway around the house. He came quickly. "How is Lydia?"

"I don't know." I felt very ignorant for not having checked. "I just heard the baby's cry." I looked beyond him, into the yard. "Where is Seth?"

"I'm sure he's right here." Mr. Bowman turned

around. "Seth said he didn't need help from me. He said he could make his own place. He wanted to dig his own tunnel on the other side of the house." He stepped farther into the backyard. "Seth! Seth! Come in now!"

Silence.

"Where is the tunnel he was to build?" Snow could cave in; Seth could be trapped.

"Over there." Mr. Bowman pointed to his right. I went into the yard. The path to the woodpile and the privy was clear. To the left the tunnel Mr. Bowman had been digging led around the house. I checked it quickly. It was dark and narrow, but the walls were strong. I reached the end easily. Seth was not there.

I turned around and ran back through the tunnel to the yard. Mr. Bowman was looking at a smaller tunnel, about Seth's height. It also led around the house, but in the opposite direction. I got down on my knees and crawled a few feet in. The tunnel was not so neat or sturdy as Mr. Bowman's, but it did not appear to have collapsed. It appeared to have stopped. I backed my way out, realizing what a strange sight I must be when I emerged, back first, snow-covered and with reddened knees and sodden petticoats. But I did not care. "Not there," I said.

We both looked down the back path I had dug that morning. I went to the end and opened the privy door. Seth was not there. But tracks through the snow led around the tall pine near the privy and toward the next street. "He went this way!" I called back to Mr. Bowman. "He shouldn't be hard to follow in the snow. You go and see if Widow Chase needs anything. I'll find Seth."

He hesitated. "Do you want me to go with you?"

"I'll be fine. He can't have gone far."

Mr. Bowman waved in agreement and returned to the house.

Chapter 13

Stopping to Home

The snow was deep, but now only light flurries were falling. Although drifts were higher than Seth's head, the bottom layers of snow were packed with ice. Seth was light. He had been able to walk on the ice and only push aside about a foot of snow to walk in. His trail led toward Summer Street.

I was heavier and taller, and walking through deep drifts was not as easy for me.

Before I reached the end of the yard my bones felt like splinters of ice.

How far could he have gone? I pushed the snow aside with my legs and hands, following the footsteps ahead of me. How long had he been away? How could Mr. Bowman not have watched him? Why did Seth decide to leave snow paths and strike out on his own into the drifts? Surely Mr. Bowman's daughter, Louisa, would never have done such a thing. It might have soiled her skirts or chilled her hands. I kept pushing through the snow. I couldn't feel my hands anymore.

Seth's trail came to an end at Summer Street. General Wood lived on Summer Street, and he had made certain it was cleared for sleighs. I looked in both directions. No sign of a small, determined, red-haired boy. The footprints I was following had blended with the sleigh tracks and the new light covering of snow.

Why would Seth have left his snow tunnel?

He had told Mr. Bowman he "could make his own place." That was the phrase Noah had used. Would Seth have gone to the river this day? There would be no one there on a snowy Christmas Sunday. But I knew nowhere else to look.

The snow flurries were getting heavier. I could hardly see the candlelit windows in the houses I passed. I walked as quickly as I could, along the edge of Summer Street to Main, and then left, down the hill toward the Sheepscot.

No one was in the streets. By now folks had long-since returned home from church and were most likely enjoying a Christmas Sunday supper.

The river was ahead of me at the bottom of the hill. It was low tide. The caps of ice covering exposed rocks had broken into patterns of lace when the waters receded. Snow covered the frozen mudflats as though it were a wide, flat meadow. Beyond, in the dark gray river waters, floes of ice scraped against each other and drifted toward the sea.

There was no sign of Seth anywhere, no footsteps to follow, and no one to ask.

I stood at the corner of Main Street and Water Street. I did not know where to turn. The snow was getting heavier. Seth was not a tall boy. He could get lost in the drifts if he ventured outside the dug paths of the streets. He had already done that once.

Two months ago he had run to Noah Brown, hoping Noah would take him to sea. But by now Noah was in Canada, I hoped, and far from Wiscasset. We had last seen him at Mrs. Nordstrom's. But Mrs. Nordstrom was at our house.

I wondered how Widow Chase and her baby were. I had not even waited to find out whether it was a boy or a girl.

Some say when one soul enters the world, another takes its leave. Please, God, I thought, please let Seth be all right.

Last December, before Seth and Ma had been sick, Ma had hoped for word from Pa by the New Year, and many days I had walked with her to Whittier's Tavern only to hear that no letters had arrived. I had gone to school last year. Last year seemed very far away.

Last year, this would not have happened. Last year Seth would not have run away.

Last year Seth would have been safe at home.

I turned down Water Street toward our old house.

The late afternoon was quiet. Falling snow smothered the sounds of ice shifting and scraping in the river and skiffs hitting the sides of wharves. Businesses and homes were closed tightly against the winter.

Where could he be?

In this cold a small boy could freeze. I shivered. I could freeze as well. I should have stopped for my cloak.

Running would warm me and save time. I had to find my brother. I had promised Ma I would look out for him. Why had he run away again?

In the silence between the sounds of my footsteps I heard something. I stopped.

There it was again.

I followed the small, choking sound, toward the building where we used to live.

Suddenly I saw him. Seth had burrowed a tiny cavelike room in a snowdrift near the stairs that had taken us up to our old room above Widow Wink's brewery. He was curled almost in a ball, like a newborn kitten, in the snow wall, and he was crying tears that were turning to ice.

I didn't want to startle him. I walked up to his hiding place and knelt down in the snow. "Seth."

He looked at me as though he hardly knew who I was. His eyelashes were covered with icy tears. "Home," he whispered.

I reached out for him. He tried to come to me, but he was too cold and stiff.

Quickly, I dug around him and lifted him out. I held him close to me and started walking back toward the center of town. I didn't say anything. Seth was safe, and I had to get both of us back to the Chases'; to warmth.

The night Ma died I had carried Seth down this same street.

I did not feel the cold. I walked through the snowy streets, past the wharves and shops. Past the houses. Up the hill toward the green, where the tall, white church steeple merged with the snow and the sky. I concentrated on putting one foot down after another.

My body was numb; I could hardly feel the weight of Seth in my arms.

Seth clung to me.

Mr. and Mrs. Bowman were waiting for us at the front door when we got to Union Street.

"Thank goodness you found him. You are both soaked and frozen. Come in by the fire and warm yourselves."

Mr. Bowman reached to take Seth out of my arms, but I shook my head. I carried Seth into the kitchen myself and put him on the floor near the fire. We were safe.

Mrs. Bowman wrapped quilts around us. All of the clothes we had been wearing were frozen with ice and snow.

"How is Widow Chase? And the baby?" I asked.

"They are fine, but Lydia's worried about you both. As soon as we saw you, I called up to her that you were coming. She'll be wanting to see you as soon as you're dry and warm."

"Seth, are you all right?"

Seth was warming up but still had not spoken.

"Do you want to see the baby?"

He nodded.

I took his hand, and we went upstairs.

Mrs. Nordstrom was going to stay the night. She was already snoring on the pallet we had put for her near Widow Chase's bedstead.

The cradle was close to the bed. Seth looked in. I started to also, but Widow Chase beckoned to me. "Come over here, Abbie." I came quietly so as not to disturb the sleeping baby or Mrs. Nordstrom. "Sit here." She patted her bed. "I was so worried about you."

I hung my head. "I'm sorry."

She raised her voice slightly and looked at Seth. "Seth, tell us. Why did you leave?"

He came over to the high bed and climbed on, tucking himself under Widow Chase's arm. "I didn't think you wanted me. Everybody was too busy with the baby to have time for me. Nobody needed me anymore." He stopped. "I wanted to go home, like Noah. I wanted to find the place right for me."

Widow Chase held him tight. "Seth, we do have to make time for the baby now, but that doesn't mean we don't love you, too." She turned to me. "Abbie, would you get three candles from the drawer in my wardrobe?"

I did so, and handed them to her.

"Seth, you take this candle. Hold it up straight. And Abbie, you take this one." She handed one candle to each of us, and put the third on the bedding. She then took the pewter candlestick holding the candle that lit her chamber from the table next to her bedstead.

"Love is like candlelight. Here is my one candle. Love only has to start with one." She reached over and lit Seth's candle with hers. "Now, I've shared my light, my love, with you, and we have much more light in the room. But my candle is as bright as it was at the start. No love was lost in giving love away." She lit my candle with hers. "I can give light, and love, to Abbie, too. And, see, there is more light in the room for all of us, and my candle is still bright." She reached for the last candle, which lay on the bedcovers. "Seth, can you hold this candle for us? Very carefully?" He nodded solemnly. "This candle is for the new baby. She can't hold her own candle yet, so she needs you to do it for her." Seth grinned, and held the candles carefully and tightly.

"Now, let us all light the baby's candle." We reached over, and all three of our candles met, their flames joined, and the fourth candle was lit. The room was filled with light.

"The first candle is still as bright, and still has as much love to share as it did at the beginning. The more love you give away, the more light there is, and the warmer and brighter the home."

"Seth"—Widow Chase turned to him—"Abbie loves you and I love you. We want you to stop running away. I want you to feel that this is your place. This is your home."

Seth looked at her and at the candles. "Can you be my ma, too? Like you're the baby's ma?"

"Your ma who gave birth to you and loved you very much is gone, Seth. I can't replace her. But I would like it very much if you could love me as a second mother."

"You can be a second mother. I think you are a good mother." Seth handed one of his candles to me and one to Widow Chase. We blew them out carefully. "I think this is a good home." He snuggled down next to Widow Chase and fell asleep almost immediately.

"Abbie, you have done so much for me since you entered this home," Widow Chase said.

"I tried to be of use."

"You did, indeed. And I hope you will continue to stay here, you and Seth. Is that all right with you, Abbie?"

"Oh, yes, Widow Chase. I would like to stay. We would both like to stay."

"It has been a very difficult year for you, I know. Your ma dying, and then your pa."

I looked at her. "I miss my ma."

"And your pa."

"Pa was often gone. I am used to his being gone. I do not really miss him. He was not a good pa to me, Widow Chase, nor a loving husband to Ma." The words tumbled out. They had been held in for such a long time.

Widow Chase blew out my candle and put all of our candles on the table. She pulled me down on the pillows next to her. Seth was on one side, and there was still space for me on the other. We were quiet for a little while. "It is all right, Abbie. You remember the good things about your ma, the way she was. And if you'll let me, I'd like to help you teach Seth the good things about being a pa so someday he will be as good a father to a child as I'm sure you will be a good mother."

My tears were dampening Widow Chase's clean pillowcase, but she didn't seem to mind.

"When I see your ma's carving of the female eider duck it makes me think that in her heart she knew all would be well with you and Seth."

I looked at Widow Chase in surprise. "The eider duck?"

"Yes. Surely you know about eider ducks?"

I shook my head. "They are sea ducks. Sometimes we see them this far upriver, but usually not."

"Yes. They are sea ducks. They live just offshore, on islands, in the heaviest of the seas and the currents. In the winter the males and females and yearling ducks all live together. But after mating in the spring the males go farther out to sea, and the females raise their young together. That's why in the summer you almost never see a male eider duck near the shore. But it is common to see several female eiders with all of their young swimming together. They swim so close that people call it a 'raft' of eiders, since from a distance it indeed looks like a raft. If anything happens to one of the females, then the others raise her ducklings as their own."

She hugged me. "I'm going to need your help, Abbie. With the baby and the house, and with the new millinery business you started for us."

I sniffed and tried to stop the tears. "I want to help."

"I know you do. It may not be like having a regular ma and pa, Abbie, but I think you and Seth and I and the baby can be a family, too."

"And not be sent away, Widow Chase?"

"Not ever sent away. I wouldn't send away family,

now, would I?" She stroked my hair. "But I am going to ask one thing of you, Abbie."

I sat up. "Yes, Widow Chase?"

"If we are going to be family, then I want you to stop calling me 'Widow Chase.' I'm not your ma, and not old enough to be, but I'd be much pleased if you would call me Lydia."

I blushed, for it sounded presumptuous. "I will try. Lydia."

"And we have another name to think of today." She gestured toward the cradle, where I could see the little wrinkled pink face of her baby wrapped in the red blankets we had embroidered.

"I would like to call my daughter Sarah Abigail. Sarah, for my friend Sally Bowman, and Abigail, for the very special young woman who will share our lives. I hope Sarah Abigail will be as strong and caring and wise as both her namesakes."

I went over to the crib and gently touched the baby's hand.

"Would you mind sharing your name, Abbie?"

I just shook my head. The tears that came now were tears of happiness.

Seth and I had found the right place for us. We had come home.

Historical Note

The seaport of Wiscasset, about fifty miles north of Portland in what is now the state of Maine, was a prosperous shipping port in the late eighteenth and early nineteenth centuries. Although Wiscasset was thirteen miles upriver from the Atlantic Ocean, the Sheepscot River was deep enough and Wiscasset Harbor large enough so that over one hundred vessels could anchor there at one time. Shipbuilding, lumbering, and trade with the West Indies and with European countries brought great wealth to the small town and made Wiscasset one of the busiest ports in New England.

In 1806, sixty-seven square-rigged vessels sailed from Wiscasset bound for international ports. James Fenimore Cooper, who became a famous American writer, sailed as a foremast hand on a ship out of Wiscasset that year. Later in his life he wrote *The Pilot,* a novel based on his years at sea.

Abbie and Seth Chambers, the Chase family, and Noah Brown are all fictional characters, although there were people like them living in early nineteenth-century Wiscasset. All of the other people and places mentioned in this book, including the orphaned moose calf, actually existed.

Celebrations and holidays mentioned in *Stopping to Home* reflect the ways in which they were celebrated in early nineteenth-century northern New England. Muster Day, a major event of each year, emphasized to citizens of the new country their responsibility to bear arms in its service when needed. The day of one's birth, although remembered in many families, was not an event to celebrate annually until the nineteenth century. Earlier, in the eighteenth century, celebrating one's own birth would have put too much emphasis on the importance of a single individual in a God-centered New England. Only royalty celebrated birth days. Thanksgiving, on the other hand, was a major family celebration, and usually included attending church and then sharing a large dinner, as families do today. Christmas was a religious holiday. The time to exchange gifts was New Year's Day. (Sally Clough Bowman asks Widow Chase to make a hat to be given to her mother on that day.)

This book was written in the house overlooking the Sheepscot where Sally Clough lived with her family on Jeremy Squam Island (now called Westport Island) before she married Jonathan Bowman.

Today Wiscasset is a beautiful village filled with stately homes reminiscent of its past days of glory.